Praise for the works

The Raven and the Banshee

The Raven and the Banshee is a great adventure set in the 1700s that brought back a lot of good memories of the old swashbuckler movies I loved as a kid—but with two female leads which is even better. I don't want to give the story away, suffice to say that there's lots of drama, lots of action, lots of betrayal, lots of brooding, lots of romance. As with Ms. Elizabeth's other novels, her main characters are engaging and well rounded and even the secondary characters felt real and fleshed out.

-*To Be Read Book Reviews*

Everything I hoped it would be... swashbuckling revenge tale with a second-chance romance to die for!! Amazing. Loved it. Bought the book!! I was looking forward to this novel since it was announced, and always fear that expectations may be too high, but not a problem; Elizabeth knocks this out of the park.

-Andi K., *NetGalley*

The Other Side of Forestlands Lake

Elizabeth (*Gallows Humor*) delivers her signature blend of lesbian romance and murder in this suspenseful outing. Paranormal YA author Willa Dunn steps into her own ghost story when she returns to her childhood summer home at Forestlands Lake. She's hoping to work on her next book and reconnect with her half-sister, rebellious teenager Nicole, but her plans are derailed by a series of spectral visitations. When Nicole gets drunk and almost drowns in the lake, Willa's childhood sweetheart, Lee Chandler, saves her. Lee, now the director of a summer camp for LGBTQ youth, and her daughter, Maggie, join together with Willa and Nicole to investigate the haunting. Between ghostly possessions and cryptic conversations with mysterious neighbors, Willa and Lee rekindle the flame that was barely allowed to flicker back when they were both closeted teens. Though the story hits some speed bumps trying to juggle the tense mystery and the lighthearted romance, the charming characters will draw in readers, and the plot ultimately hangs together nicely. Fans of romantic suspense are sure to be pleased.

-Publishers Weekly

The author uses great descriptions and innocuous little details to give the community surrounding the lake a disturbing personality. This is a nice juxtaposition with the giddiness Willa and Lee feel over being reunited. I enjoyed losing myself in a paranormal story. I'm pretty set in my ways about sticking to the romance genre, but this was a nice change of pace. The book is well paced, and it's spooky enough to raise the hair on the back of your neck without making you need to sleep with the lights on.

-The Lesbian Review

It took only one book by Carolyn Elizabeth for me to decide that she was a must-read author. This is her third and it proves true again. I love Elizabeth's stories but even if I didn't, I'd read her books for the characters. She makes me fall in love with all of them.

There are many layers to this book, and so we don't get one mystery but two. Well-thought, complex and thrilling mysteries. Everything came as a surprise yet still made complete sense (in a paranormal way).

Carolyn Elizabeth is proving that she could write any genre and I'd want to read it. In this book, you get romance, paranormal and mystery all in one, with each element being as important and as well-crafted.

-Les Rêveur

Dirt Nap

Yes! This is how you write a sequel, you make it even better than the first. For those readers that were hoping for more of

Thayer and Corey, including their relationship, you won't be disappointed. Their connection keeps growing, the chemistry is in your face and every romantic scene is just as good as the most exciting scenes in the book. All the story lines of this book really hit for me. From a little relationship angst to Corey's big problem with a trusted friend, there was always something going on that kept me flipping these pages.

-Lex Kent's Reviews, *goodreads*

This is a perfect sequel to *Gallows Humor* and met all of my... high expectations. Sometimes sequels can be disappointing, but not this one. We have the same mystery, intrigue, and romance that we found in the first book. Corey, Thayer, and all the secondary characters are just as likable and easy to connect with. The romance is still as sweet, and it was fun seeing the two grow together through all the trials they had to endure. It was also fun meeting a few new characters and watching them develop. Ms. Elizabeth not only has the knowledge she needs in pathology and medicine for this story, she also shines in character development. This is what makes both of these books so great.

-Betty H., *NetGalley*

I must admit that this is the second time that I was blown away with this author's captivating writing style. She has really outdone herself with this story because she gave me a riveting romantic thriller that has so many entertaining and laugh-out-loud moments embedded within it. This story kept me glued to my Kindle and hungry for more priceless wisecracks from Corey and Thayer. Even though Carolyn Elizabeth did a wonderful job of filling in some of the details and facts from her first book, I would strongly advise you to read *Gallows Humor* before you read this story so that you would get to know more about these lovely characters.

-*The Lesbian Review*

Gallows Humor

At this very moment, my coffee cup is raised in Carolyn Elizabeth's honor because she gave me the perfect blend of an angst-filled, budding romance with endless humor and an enthralling murder mystery that kept me up way past my bedtime. I still can't get over the fact that this story is her debut novel because Carolyn Elizabeth has knocked my fluffy bedroom socks off with her flawless writing and the witty and entertaining dialogue between the characters along with the vivid descriptions of the Jackson City Memorial Hospital and environs.

If you're looking for a story that will keep you on the edge of your seat and have you doubled over with laughter, then this is definitely the story for you!

-The Lesbian Review

I always enjoy reading good debuts. It gets me excited to find new authors. I would recommend this book to just about anyone. I think people will enjoy this read. I hope there is a book two because I will be reading it. Almost forgot, I also like the oddball title of the book.

-Lex Kent's Reviews, *goodreads*

KISS
SHOT

Carolyn Elizabeth

About the Author

Carolyn Elizabeth is a Goldie Award-winning author of Sapphic fiction where serious camp meets upbeat macabre.

She enjoys weaving elements of her colorful and diverse life experiences into her romantic blend fiction.

KISS
SHOT

Carolyn Elizabeth

BELLA
BOOKS
2023

Bella Books, Inc.
P.O. Box 10543
Tallahassee, FL 32302

Printed in the United States of America on acid-free paper.

First Edition - 2023

Editor: Ann Roberts
Cover Designer: Heather Honeywell

ISBN: 978-1-64247-384-1

Acknowledgments

Thank you to Bella Books for your continued belief in me and the stories I enjoy telling. Many thanks to my editor, Ann Roberts, for your continued support and counsel. It is always appreciated.

Thank you to my brother from another mother, Luc, for giving this one an advance read and giving me the appropriate amount of shit for it.

I don't know if I've explicitly stated this anywhere, but thus far, my books are all inspired by, or based loosely on, my real-life experiences.

Many of the deaths in the Curtis and Reynolds series are inspired by autopsies I've assisted on. The *Banshee* is based on the HM Bark *Endeavour* Replica, which I had the pleasure of sailing on for a week twenty-five years ago. Forestlands Lake was inspired by the people and landscape (not the ghosts) of a family community in which I nannied for a young girl when I was in high school.

In keeping with that, *Kiss Shot* was inspired by a woman I dated in my early twenties. The limerick I wrote for her. I thought it would be funny to include it. She was the 1996 ACUI Women's National Billiards Champion.

In order to share in the things that made her happy, I had to learn my way around a pool table. For my twenty-second birthday she gifted me with my very own pool cue, which I still have.

In the grand scheme of things, it wasn't a long period of time in my life, but I remember it well and fondly. Except for that time I broke my hand trying to punch out her car window.

The bikers I made up.

Enjoy.

Your sweet stroke affects me like wine.
Your break sends chills down my spine.
Your moves on the table
were how you were able
to make me want to make your heart mine.

CHAPTER ONE

"Where the hell are you?" I muttered.

Leaning toward the windshield and squinting into the setting spring sun was in no way helping me find the young woman I was looking for, but it did help me to not run over the woman crossing the street in front of me. I screeched to a stop and waved an apology. She gave me the finger.

Turning the radio down didn't locate my quarry either, but having it on was against regs, so maybe I could do one thing right today. I cruised through the industrial area of Albany, New York, again. The same streets I'd been over twice already in the last half hour. "Where the hell are you?"

At every stop sign, at every street corner in front of every mini-mart, groups of young men and women pulled up their hoods or lowered their hats, jammed hands into pockets and scattered. An unmarked black police-issue Ford Taurus wasn't nearly as subtle as the city officials liked to believe. The low-profile puck antennae on the back helped, but there was no hiding the driver's side spotlight and bull bar on the front grille.

What definitely didn't help was that my self-imposed work uniform looked like I raided Olivia Benson's early *SVU* seasons closet. I got pegged for a cop a mile away even without the car. Even so, I didn't mix up my wardrobe. I couldn't imagine anything worse than actually *deciding* what I was going to wear to work every day. Department store charcoal chinos and V-neck sweaters over fitted white T-shirts—every damn day.

Turning east gave me a break from the sun just in time to spy the pale, skinny girl in ripped jeans and stained gray hoodie shuffling along. She was hunched over as if the oversize canvas bag slung across her chest weighed a hundred pounds.

"Gotcha." I blooped the siren to get her attention.

She whirled around and stared wide-eyed before taking off down the street much faster than her previous gait would have suggested she could move.

"Shit, don't run." I gunned it up the road, bouncing through potholes deep enough to rattle my teeth, and barely making the stop to follow her when she darted down a narrow alley.

"Come on, kid, gimme a break." I jumped the curb and threw the car in park, actually remembering to close and lock the doors this time before taking off down the alley after her. If I lost another two-way radio or got another laptop smashed, the captain was gonna have my ass.

My boots pounded over the cracked pavement as I gained ground, my right hand on my sidearm at my hip to keep it still, not because I had any intention of drawing it. She ran down the alley toward a high chain-link fence. She probably hadn't had a decent meal in days and was slowing fast. "If you make me climb that fence, I'm gonna be pissed!"

She leapt for the fence and scrambled up, but wasn't anywhere near the top when I caught up to her and dragged her off by the ankle. "That's enough, we're done!" I was more winded than I would ever admit. Butch black logger boots were great for kicking in doors and kicking asses, not so much for a full sprint.

"Get your damn hands off me, pig!" She got her feet under her and took a wild swing, connecting solidly with my ear.

"Ow, Jesus! What the fuck?" I gripped her by the arm and spun her toward the fence, pushing her up against it and kicking her legs apart.

"You told me to play hard to get, Lucky." She snickered while I pulled her bag off her and gave her a cursory pat down.

"You punched me in the ear, Sky." I shook my head and pulled handcuffs from the case clipped at my lower back and cuffed her loosely with her hands in front. My ear was hot and throbbing.

She scowled. "Really, Lucky, cuffs? You're the one who told me to make you work for it."

"There's no one even watching right now." I marched her back down the alley with a hand around her arm.

"There's always someone watching," she said under her breath.

As was our usual custom, I drove twenty-five minutes to Schenectady and pulled around to the back of the Mattress Warehouse a block from Denny's. Sky got out at the empty loading dock and walked the rest of the way to the restaurant while I took a lap around the block, making sure there was no one we needed to worry about. She wasn't wrong. There were eyes everywhere and no such thing as being too cautious. She was already at a table at the back of the restaurant, near the restrooms and away from the windows, when I caught up to her.

Denny's was packed with teenagers and seniors. No one noticed us besides our server, who was paid to pay attention to us, but even then, I doubted they could give an accurate description. I ordered a club sandwich, fries, and a water which was the only thing I could stomach here and Sky Kingston ordered her usual, T-bone and eggs with a side of bacon and pancakes. Probably the only time she ate any meat was when I paid. She was not shy about taking full advantage of free refills on her Coke either.

She disappeared to the bathroom for a long time, no doubt washing up more than just her hands and her face, stuffing her oversize bag with anything that wasn't nailed down—

toilet paper, paper towels and liquid soap from the dispenser. She kept a small plastic bottle in her bag just for that. She was even thinner than usual and probably didn't weigh much more than a hundred pounds. Her skin was pale and tight over her cheekbones, but there were no visible lesions. Her lank blond hair could use a wash, but her eyes were clear and her teeth still intact. I didn't have to worry too much today.

She looked in better shape than I had when I'd first been rousted by the cops. Spending any amount of time with Sky always brought up the memories of my blessedly short time on the streets. I was fourteen when my drug-addicted mother's third boyfriend in as many years tried to put his hands on me and I took off with nothing but the clothes I was wearing. Six months later and I got busted in a flophouse drug raid—filthy and infested, high as a kite, going down on some lowlife for half a bag of Doritos and a warm beer.

The detective who found me, Angela Curran, wrapped me in a blanket, got me a hot meal, a toothbrush, and a desperately needed shower. Instead of just handing me off to Children's Services she made sure I got placed in a decent group home. She told me repeatedly how *lucky* I was that she found me before something worse happened. And how the word was only one letter away from my name, Lucy, as if I couldn't spell. The name stuck and I was more than happy for one less thing to remind me of my old life and the woman who called herself my mother.

With Angela's help I got my GED, associate's degree, and went on to do a four-year degree in three years at John Jay College of Criminal Justice. Next came the academy, patrol, and detective by thirty. I now called Angela Curran, Captain.

Sky Kingston may have a tougher time of it being an adult and having the hurdles of her criminal record to overcome, but I wanted the same chance for her and was going to do everything in my power to see it happen. At least for now, I could get her help from the department as long as she stayed signed on as a confidential informant and produced some actionable intelligence.

Be cool. Be cool. Sky returned at the same time as our food and I forced myself to wait until she got something into her belly before checking in with her. "How ya been, Sky?"

"Good, uh-huh," she said around a mouthful of pancakes drowning in syrup and butter.

"Yeah? You been using?"

Her eyes narrowed and she dropped her fork with a clatter, sitting back against the booth. "What the hell, Lucky? You want me to dig in with the fucking Rat Lords MC for you, but 'spect me to stay clean? Sure, yeah, no problem. Dudes be sittin' around blowin' rails and I'll be all 'Nah, not feelin' it, thanks though.' You tryna get me killed?"

I raised my hands in apology. "No, of course not. I'm sorry. I just worry about you."

She stared at me for another long moment before shrugging and going back to her food. "No one's worried 'bout me for a minute."

"Well, get used to it."

"What about you? You been playin' at all?"

"Pool? Just at the bar. Since making detective last year and being assigned to Street Crimes, I've been tits deep in the Rat Lords task force. I don't have time for anything else."

"That time you took me to Golden Cue in Troy. That was dope. Wish we could hit that again. Those motherfuckers' faces when you beat 'em. So dope."

That night had been fun and nice to see her smile and laugh for a little while. Almost looking like the young woman she could have been if not hardened by her circumstances. "I'm glad you had a good time. We can totally do that again. Whenever you want." I let her eat in peace for several minutes but couldn't hide my anxious tension.

"What?" she asked without looking up from her plate.

"You *know* what. Did you get it?"

She wiped her mouth and sat back. "Got somethin' for me?"

I slid a fifty-dollar bill across the table.

She eyed it. "That it?"

"No. What's the address?"

"It's in Mendanville. Forty Baldwin Street."

"See how easy that was?"

"Yeah, fuckin' right. Know what I had to do for that addy?"

I handed over three more fifties, making a note to myself to write up the paperwork to get reimbursed from the department, though they'd probably only approve half of the two hundred I gave her. "I can imagine."

"No. You really can't." She jammed the bills in her pocket.

Whatever it was, I suspected it involved a whole bottle of mouthwash after. As much as I hated thinking about that time in my life, I sure had to draw on it a lot to do my job. Maybe not the most well-thought plan to go into Street Crimes. But it was where I felt I could make the most difference. "You know I've been where you are."

She snorted, her right hand going to her necklace, her fingers worrying at the gold *S* hanging from the short gold chain. I'd never seen her without it. Fiddling with it was the tell that she was getting agitated. "You played at it a few months. It weren't your life."

"It doesn't have to be yours either, Sky." I reached across the table for her hand but she moved away. "I'm just trying to help you. You know that, right?"

Her jaw clenched. "As long as I help you, first. That it?"

Her words hit home and I jerked back as far as the booth would allow. She wasn't wrong. I was single with no family to speak of and I lived simply. I was doing okay on a cops' salary, but I didn't have the resources to really help her on my own. It had to come from the department. "It's almost over, I promise."

"Heard that before."

That stung. She knew how to get at me. Every damn time. "I'm sorry. I wish I could do more."

Her expression softened, her mouth twisting into the beginning of a smile. "It's all good, Lucky. I know you tryin'. More than anyone else ever did for me. Hey, um…"

"What's up?"

She grew uncharacteristically emotional and started rubbing at the necklace again. "I been thinkin'. You think maybe, um… You think you could help me find my sister?"

"Your sister?" I didn't know she had a sister.

"Yeah, um, she's three years older. Half-sister. Different dudes. When my mom got busted we got split up. An aunt or somethin' on her dad's side took her in, I think. I was only six."

"What's her name?"

"Brooke. Don't know her last name. She gave me this necklace. It's real gold, maybe. Sure she lifted it, but whatever. She looked out for me though, when things got real bad at home and I just…"

Her story just drifted off and her expression turned hard again. I wasn't going to get any more out of her. If she even knew. Without a last name, I'd have to start back at her mother's arrest record or maybe Children's Services could help me. It would be a slog. "Yeah, sure, Sky, I'll see what I can do."

"Thanks, Lucky. I gotta go."

"Let me pay and I'll give you a ride back to the city."

"Nah, thanks. I'll bus it. I got some stops to make." She slipped her bag over her shoulder and grabbed a triangle of sandwich from my plate. I pretended not to see when she slipped the steak knife up the sleeve of her hoodie. "Thanks for the eats."

"Any time. Hey, you wanna catch up in a couple of days? See if you learned anything more and I'll tell you what I can about the stash house plans."

She smirked. "Why don't you see if you can hunt me down at the underpass."

"Oh, no." I grimaced. "Anywhere but—"

"That's where my peeps at. Gotta work for it remember?" Her smirk grew.

"Fuck. Fine." I shook my head in resignation. "Hey, Sky. Thanks for the address. It's the break we've been looking for."

"Yeah, well, do some good. For once."

I laughed. "Listen, Sky, maybe lay low this week and see where this goes, okay?"

"Thought you just said you wanted me to learn more."

I winced. More information was always better. "Just...be careful, okay?"

"Sure. See ya when I see ya, Lucky."

CHAPTER TWO

"Did you get it?" Detective Ray Keller, my friend since the academy and partner for the last year, asked when I blew back into the department and headed straight for Captain Curran's office.

He was the Norman Reedus to my Mariska Hargitay. He had an unhealthy obsession with Daryl Dixon from *The Walking Dead*—long hair hanging in his eyes and constant three-day stubble dressed up with a rumpled dirtbag-style shirt and skinny tie. "Yeah, I got it."

I slammed into the body that put itself directly into my path with a surprised grunt. I pushed back off him and into Ray behind me. "What the hell, Clay?"

Clay Craig was my age but his receding hair, which he kept closely cropped, suggested otherwise. He compensated by cultivating an enviable cop-stache. Except he wasn't a cop. Everyone knew he'd entered the academy on two separate occasions and that he'd been dismissed both times. No one knew why. Couldn't have been because he couldn't pass PT. Dude was huge. He worked now as Captain Curran's administrative assistant by day and a private security guard by night.

He wagged a beat-up Folgers can at me. "You haven't put in for coffee this month, Sorin."

"Because I don't drink it."

He scowled. "What cop doesn't drink coffee?"

"This one." I tried to edge around him, but he blocked me. "Seriously, dude?"

"I got it." Ray crammed a five into the can over my shoulder and Clay went about his business without another word.

"What is with that guy? He's always in my damn way," I muttered, and continued across the room.

"Takes his job seriously, I guess." Ray shrugged.

"Buying coffee isn't even his job."

"It isn't? Whose is it?"

"How the hell should I know? I don't drink coffee."

"Then how do you know it's not—"

I cut him off with a sharp wave, knocked sharply on the captain's door, and let myself in without an invitation. "I got the address, Ang." I straightened and cleared my throat when I saw she was in a meeting with another team from the Street Crimes Unit. The two senior members of the Rat Lords MC task force, Sergeant Al Forbes and his partner, Detective Michelle Monroe, made it very clear they didn't approve of my inclusion on the team or my personal relationship with the captain. "I'm sorry for interrupting." Was I, though?

They turned to glare at me. Forbes was tall and bald and Monroe kept her hair pulled back painfully tight from her broad face. She was as fair as he was dark, but they were both heavy and muscular—their partnership spilling over into weight training.

When I first started with the task force, I was sure I'd be pals with Monroe, the only other woman besides the captain, but that had not been the case at all. Monroe, five years my senior, was chilly from the jump, had no interest in mentoring, and spoke to me like I was a high-schooler doing a ride-along for a class project.

It was good I didn't have my heart set on making any deep personal connections within the team. The only other cops we worked with on the regular were a pair pulled from patrol as needed, Lyons and Neal. Phil Lyons was a bulky, twice-divorced father of four with dark, deep-set eyes, bushy brows and pock-marked face. His twenty-something partner, Brian Neal, had white-blond hair, pale blue eyes, and boyish good looks he balanced out by being an absolute dickhead at every opportunity. Except for Ray, our oddball group didn't leave a lot of room for backyard barbeques on days off. Not that Ray and I had ever even barbequed. We were the go out together kind of friends, not come over and hang out kind of friends.

We waited patiently in the doorway until Captain Angela Curran waved us in. Her wavy black hair was held back in a clip, putting her sharp, ageless features on full display. Her brown skin stood out against the white silk collar of her blouse beneath her suit jacket. "Well, you're here now. Saves me the trouble of calling you all back together. Let's hear what you got."

"Forty Baldwin Street in Mendanville. It's the stash house we've been looking for." I was way too excited to play it cool, finally contributing something solid to this case.

Captain Curran pursed her lips, her gaze holding mine for a long moment before flicking to Forbes and Monroe. "Get on it. Pull in Lyons and Neal for extra boots on the ground. I want round-the-clock surveillance until we have enough for a warrant. Then we go in. No mistakes."

"Right, boss," Forbes rumbled and stalked toward the door without sparing me a glance, let alone an atta-girl.

Ray jumped out of the way of the big man, but I refused to move and almost got spun all the way around when his meaty shoulder bumped mine on his way out the door. I heard Monroe snicker as she followed him out. Bitch.

"Come on, Lucky. We don't want Lyons and Neal to get first pick of the shift rotation," Ray said, halfway out the door.

"Lucy, a word, please." Captain Curran was the only one who still called me that despite being the one who coined my nickname.

"Go ahead. I'll catch up." I waved Ray off. "What's up?"

"Your name came up when I met with the chief yesterday afternoon."

"That can't be good." I racked my brain. Late paperwork? Insubordination? Not drinking coffee? "What did I do, now?"

"Close the door."

I did and dropped into a chair across from her. Angela settled back behind her desk. "The mayoral election is coming up."

I accessed my mental calendar and frowned. "In like a year."

"Like I said, coming up. As you well know, Deborah Kinney is Albany's first female mayor and it's a big deal."

"I get it."

"The Rat Lords are a problem and if we can't get them under control it's going to go badly for her come election time. The new ADA is making noise about announcing his candidacy. Rumor has it, he's already building a platform that Kinney can't get it done and he's using the Rat Lords' escalating crimes as his prime example."

"The new ADA? That little weaselly punk? What's his name, Slicker? Slither? Slather?"

Angela almost smiled. "Slater. He's got a lot of friends and a lot of momentum. Policing should be above politics and I'll deny ever having said this, but if we ever want to see another woman in elected office, she needs a big win."

My eyes rolled painfully. "Work twice as hard as a man and all that shit?"

"You and I both know it's true. Especially on the force. Or in politics. As a woman you have to get real results and have an impeccable record along the way."

"Yeah, Ang, I know. And I get that you and the mayor are pals, but I also know we're doing everything we can to—"

"Not everything. We can do more. Get closer."

I stared at her for a long moment, working through the possibilities. "You want to send someone inside?"

"Chief Lee's suggestion. He's held the reins for less than a year and feeling the pressure, too. He has his share of detractors who would be happy to lay the blame of the rise in organized crime at his feet. And they wouldn't be wrong. It's time to get creative on this, Lucy."

"Okay, so send someone undercover." She didn't need my permission. I was missing something and waited expectantly for the other shoe to drop. It did in the form of her intense prolonged stare and the muscle in her jaw jumping. I barked a laugh. "Who? Me?"

"I won't order you and depending on what we can turn up in this stash house, we likely won't even need to. But the question has been raised about the possibilities."

My mind reeled, thoughts pinballing off each other and making my head throb. It would be terrifying. It could get me killed. And thrilling. It would be great for my career. I had some undercover experience from my years on patrol when the guys from narcotics needed to round out a UC operation with a couple of women for backup. Women were always easy to explain away as girlfriends and never looked at twice. I had the instinct for it. And the nerves. I could protect Sky, or even better, get her out. I wouldn't need her anymore if I was inside. "Why me?"

"Why do you think?"

"Because I'm your best detective?" I batted my lashes.

Angela shook her head but couldn't entirely hide her smile. "Why *else* do you think?"

I looked away, my mouth twisting into the expression of disgust I couldn't help make whenever I thought of my childhood and what I had to do to survive. Shoulda gone into Cyber Crimes, then.

"That's right," she said softly. "You know these people, Lucy. I don't need cop skills, or, not *just* cop skills. I need street skills. You can get inside their heads, play the game. Literally."

"I don't know, Ang."

"Just think about it. If we need to, we'll revisit the conversation after we do the work to take down the stash house."

"You want me to be part of the raid? If I go in there and bust up that house, Rat Lords will know I'm a cop. I'll get killed before I even make it past the front door if I try and get in on the inside after that."

"Of course, you're going to be a part of the raid. This is your intel. Your bust as much as it is anyone's."

"An undercover op won't be an option for me after, though."

"Maybe." Angela frowned and all of a sudden couldn't meet my eyes. "Maybe not."

Her vagaries and puzzling nonanswers were triggering my bullshit meter. "You know something else? What is it?"

She opened her mouth as if to speak and clearly thought better of whatever she was going to say. "Just, trust me, Lucy."

That didn't help. "You know, I do."

She nodded sharply. "Let's just stick to the plan for now. Execute this raid, get the evidence we need and we won't have to worry about sending anyone under. I know I don't have to tell you this conversation stays between us. No one knows about this. No one."

"Yeah, of course." I knew she meant Ray, too. Partners told each other everything. They had to trust without reservation. It would be hard keeping this from him and I didn't like it. And I sensed something else was going on. "What aren't you telling me?"

"That will be all, Detective Sorin."

My lips thinned at her dismissal, but I knew better than to push her. Angela, I could sometimes wheedle information out of, but Captain Curran was ice cold and expert at her job. "Yes, ma'am."

Copper Jacks, the local cop bar, was business as usual. The three bar-size pool tables in the back were full. Pool had always been the go-to de-stressor I could rely on to clear my mind. There were no gray areas and moral fine lines—just physics, skill, strategy, and maybe some shit-talking. Definitely some shit-talking.

There was an old donated table in my group home and I had taken to it like I'd been born for it. When not playing, I watched Allison Fisher videos. For my college graduation Angela bought me a twelve-hundred-dollar, custom bird's-eye maple cue with abalone diamond inlays and brass trim rings. It was beautiful and the singular luxury item I owned. Except to me it was a necessity. Playing pool calmed the clown car of my mind like nothing else. Tonight, though, I just wanted to have a drink with Ray.

"What did Curran want?" he asked.

I spun my bottle around and picked at the label. "Just about the raid. Good work on the intel. That kind of shit."

His eyes narrowed. "She couldn't say that in front of me?"

I took a long drink and swallowed. "And some other personal stuff. You know how she sometimes gets with me."

"Uh-huh." He wasn't buying it.

"Hey, ladies." Neal banged a pitcher of beer on the table, sloshing it everywhere, and a single glass. It was apparently all for him. He spun the chair around and straddled it like the tool he was.

Ray leaned back in his chair to put some distance between them. "Thought you'd be doing overnights in Mendanville."

Neal cupped his hands around his mouth and shouted, "No overtime!"

A couple of officers nearby laughed and raised a glass in his direction.

Lyons joined us, sitting in a chair properly and adding a few fresh beers for the table. I helped myself to one. "The loo's cracking down on the budget. We'll take our turn on overnights, but we worked a full shift already. Forbes and Monroe are on tonight," he said.

"We're on tomorrow night," I added for something to say.

Lyons clinked his bottle with mine. "Nice work on gettin' that address. This could be the beginning of the end of the rat fucks."

"I'll drink to that," Ray said.

Neal looked worried. "But won't that mean we'll be back to patrol full time? No more stakeouts and raids?"

I rolled my eyes. He would rather this investigation go on forever so he could keep playing action hero and impress the bleached badge bunnies he was so fond of. His favorite, Dani, was on her way over to the table with extra red on her lips and swing in her hips. "It means we've done our job and rid the city of a dangerous criminal organization. I'm sure you'll get a commendation."

His eyes brightened. "Really?"

"No," Ray and I said in unison and laughed.

Even Lyons had an amused smirk. "Just quarters in the karma bank, partner."

"Fuck you guys." He scowled and grabbed his pitcher as he got up, far more interested now in what the young woman was whispering in his ear.

CHAPTER THREE

The next night we were late to relieve Lyons and Neal at the stash house because Ray insisted the coffee at the Starbucks on Western Avenue was the best of any coffee shop in the city, including other Starbucks. Apparently, he wasn't the only one to think so, and even at eleven at night the line was ten cars deep. Where could all these people possibly be going that they needed coffee at nearly midnight?

At least our requisitioned surveillance vehicle was a choice get, a 2018 Toyota Corolla with no bells and whistles and nothing to give it away as police issue. Not so nice that it would stand out on the street, but new enough it didn't yet reek of stale smoke and fast-food farts. Ray tried calling Lyons again to let him know we were here and get their report on the day shift.

"What the hell are those fools doing? They better not be sleeping. Do you see them?" he grumbled as we drove down Baldwin Street.

"Nope." I pulled into a spot three houses down from the stash house with an unobstructed view of the front and killed the engine. "And if I drive by again we're gonna get made. There's three cars in the driveway and lights on in the front window."

It was a run-down, nondescript bungalow on a run-down, nondescript residential street in the town of Mendanville, New York, a working-class poor suburb of Albany. Mendanville had its own police force, but not one equipped to handle the influx of gangs, guns, and drugs moving upstate from New York City. Albany PD had its own unit designed to handle organized street crime in all of Albany County. Our task force was designated specifically to build the case against the Rat Lords Motorcycle Club, which had been cementing their status in the guns and drug trade in the Capital Region since moving into the area two years ago.

"I'm gonna try Neal." He jabbed at his phone and put it on speaker. After three rings there was a brief moment of silence followed by music and loud chatter. "Neal? What the hell? Where are you, man?"

"You were late." Neal laughed at something unintelligible.

Ray's eyes widened. "A few minutes. Jesus. Did you just leave? Are you at the bar?"

"Twenty minutes. And there was nothing to report. So, yeah, we're at the bar."

"Jesus Christ, those fucking idiots," I muttered and then louder, "How would you know how late we were? It takes at least forty minutes to get to the bar from here. You left before the end of your shift, asshole. There are three cars in the driveway, Neal. Did you see them arrive? Who got out of them? Did you get photos?"

"How the hell should I know? It's your shift." The line went dead.

My jaw ached from gritting my teeth. "That little prick. I'm gonna—"

"What? File a report? No, you're not. That's career suicide." Ray tossed his phone onto the dash.

"You're not pissed?"

"Hell, yeah, I am. I can't stand those jerk-offs." He reached into the back seat and pulled out the Nikon digital SLR. We were close enough not to need an additional lens to document the cars and plates. "You gonna start running tags or what? Don't got all night."

"Yeah, you do." I flipped open the laptop. "Ready when you are."

"Black, late-model Ford Mustang soft top…"

Three hours later, two of the cars had left, leaving only the Mustang. The other two tags came back registered to college kids with no record—yet. That would change pretty quick if they were making a habit of frequenting Rat Lords' drug dens. We logged the information for the report. There were occasional silhouettes passing back and forth in front of the window, but no one we could identify. The Mustang's plates had come up stolen. This could be interesting depending on who came out and got in it.

Ray slurped on his coffee. "Why aren't there any Harleys?"

"If they parked the bikes in the driveway we probably would have found this place a lot sooner."

He shrugged. "I guess."

"There's an alley that runs behind this entire street with garages and storage. They probably get in that way. No way for us to surveil from back there."

"Right. We should get a drone."

"We can't even get the vending machine fixed."

We fell silent again for half an hour and my eyes drooped. Eating too much put me to sleep. Drinking anything and I'd have to piss with nowhere to go. I tried using a bottle once and it did not go well. Picture putting your thumb over a running garden hose. Overnights sucked and I… "Whoa." I jerked up in my seat when the front door opened and a man headed to the stolen car.

Ray frowned at the house and snapped a series of photos. "Is that who I think it is?"

"Only if you're thinking it's Zak Mackey." I banged away at the laptop.

Ray snorted from behind the camera. "Didn't realize he was out again."

"Released last month from his *second* stint for possession with intent to sell and on parole for three years. Now he's here in a stolen car and probably got his pockets stuffed with blow."

"We should call it in."

I waited for Mackey to pull out and drive to the end of the block before starting the car. We were facing the right direction and at two in the morning there were few other cars to worry about getting between us.

"What the hell are you doing? We can't just leave."

I kept my eyes on Mackey's taillights as he turned right, heading toward the 787 onramp, which would take us back into the city. "We can, if scooping up Mackey gets us the intel we need. Grand theft, possession, and I'll put money on him being armed. That's a hat trick of a parole violation *and* his third strike. He'll tell us everything we want to know." Mackey was stopped ahead at a light and I accelerated to catch up before the light turned green.

"But we got no siren and no lights. How are you gonna— Jesus, Lucky!" Ray threw his hands against the dash.

I slammed on the brakes too late and smacked into the back of the Mustang hard enough to push it into the intersection. I kept it below fifteen miles per hour and prayed the airbags wouldn't deploy. They didn't. A moment later the Mustang's door flew open and Zak Mackey appeared, massaging his neck while he walked to the back to inspect the damage, swearing at us the entire way.

Ray glared at me. "Curran's gonna be pissed."

I grinned back. "Nah, she'll be fine. Let's go get our boy."

* * *

I exited 787 to Broadway and rolled the window down, slowing beneath the cloverleaf to the Dunn Memorial Bridge. Busted cardboard and trash littered the road. Ripped tents in vacant lots flapped in the breeze that stank of urine and rotten food against the backdrop of the unique scent of the Hudson River. I pulled over but left the car running. I wasn't planning to stay long. I could feel the eyes on us from the intact tents and more robust appliance boxes at the top of the steep concrete ramp, jammed beneath the underpass where they were best protected from the elements. An old man—or woman—shuffled past on the road, pushing a rusted, three-wheeled shopping cart laden with salvaged items. It was heartbreaking and infuriating and I hated it here.

"Why am I here again?" Ray grimaced, watching the person move on, leaving a trail of collected cans dropping through the hole in the bottom of the cart in their wake.

"I need to talk to Sky and I need you to stay with the car."

"Why?" Ray started to put his window down and changed his mind when a close-quarters blast of rank air made its way in.

"So, nothing happens to it, numnuts."

He snorted. "I mean why do you need to talk to Sky? Thanks to Zak Mackey we have everything we need. The raid is on."

"I told her I'd keep her in the loop if I could."

"You don't owe her anything, you know? She works for us and gets paid. And don't think I don't know you hook her up out of your own pocket."

"What's it to you?" Ray could be a selfish prick.

"Nothing, man. I just…you just…"

"What?"

He sighed and looked away. "You get too close, Lucky. Care too much."

"I didn't realize caring was a character flaw."

"It's not. Jesus, man, why you gotta make everything so damn hard? I just don't want to see you get hurt."

I winced. Maybe selfish wasn't the right word. "You don't have to worry about me, Ray. I'm fine."

"Yeah, sure. You know where to find her?"

"Gotta pretty good idea," I said halfway out the door. "Back in a few."

I trotted up the steep ramp, careful not to put a foot wrong on the cracked and crumbling spots and break an ankle. Or worse, go ass over teakettle back to the bottom. A busted leg would heal. I'd never recover if Ray saw me fall.

I'd only met Sky here twice before even though she frequented the spot often. There was a group she liked to hang with, people her own age. They were safe—or *safer*. They were a little more pulled together than the usual street kids, had a bit of money, food, cigarettes, and better booze. I didn't see any of them now, though.

I risked calling for her, raising my voice to be heard over the traffic from the bridge above me. "Sky? You around?"

A sharp scrape and rustle from deep under the bridge had my heart pounding. I bent to peer into the dark. It smelled really bad back there—piss and vomit. I did not want to go farther. I waited for the rumble of cars overhead to quiet so I could be heard without shouting. There was more shuffling and a flash of movement. "Sky is that you? You okay?"

"…the hell way from me…" she slurred.

It was Sky, I was sure, and she sounded bad. I glanced back at the car. Ray committed to having the window down, probably to keep an eye on me, and was watching me with a frown. I gave him a wave.

"Sky, it's Lucky. Come on out and I'll get you some help."

"Don't want your help."

"Some food then," I tried. "Just come out so we can talk."

"Nothin' to say to you, bitch!" she screeched.

I jerked back at her venom, my hand instinctively going to my weapon when she moved closer, the acrid smell of urine and vomit coming with her. I could see her better now. Her hair hung lank in her face and she was jerking and scratching at her arms. Her clothes were filthy and she was barefoot. How the hell did she get so strung out? I just saw her. The car door opened down below and I could feel Ray's eyes on me.

"Lucky?" he called.

I waved a hand behind me to get him to stay back. "Please, come out all the way so I can see you."

She stilled, her arms dropping to her sides.

"Please, Sky, you're scaring me."

"You should be scared," she hissed and launched herself at me with an inhuman shriek.

I sucked in a sharp breath and stepped back, thumbing the stop snap on my holster with my right hand and raising my left arm to protect myself from the flash of metal in her hand. She slammed into me and the sharp pain across my left forearm was nothing compared to the pain in my heart at the feral rage pouring off her as we hit the ground. I skidded several feet down the ramp with Sky on top of me, her wild arms battering at me furiously, but few blows landing.

"Stop!" Ray roared from below us.

I craned my head around awkwardly. He was making his way up, weapon drawn. "Stand down, Ray!" I grunted when Sky's right fist connected with my cheek. "Sky, stop!"

"Get off of her now! I will shoot you," Ray warned.

He meant it and I would do the same in his position. Fear for Sky sent a jolt of adrenaline to every muscle and I surged up, throwing her off me and getting between them, arms splayed in both directions. "No, Ray. Hold your fire."

Sky crouched, wild-eyed and panting. She didn't seem to even recognize me. She snarled, baring her teeth, and bolted back up the ramp and through a hole in the chain-link fence separating the underpass from the bridge above.

My hand flew to my mouth, but the sounds of screeching tires and crunching metal never came. Just the constant drone of cars overhead. She apparently wasn't so out of her mind she ran into traffic.

"Jesus Christ, Lucky." Ray holstered his weapon. "That scared the hell outta me. You okay?"

I exhaled a shaky breath. "Yeah, I'm okay, thanks."

He gestured to my arm. "That looks nasty. That from the fall?"

Blood was dripping off the tips of my fingers from the ragged slice across my forearm. As soon as I eyed it, the pain kicked in and I sucked a breath through my teeth. "She cut me."

Ray jerked his tie off and handed it to me. "With what? A busted bottle?"

I wound his tie around my arm. "A steak knife."

CHAPTER FOUR

The good news is, I'm a fast healer. In only a few days the burning ache in my arm was mostly gone. No doubt I could have used several stitches, but I had no patience for waiting rooms and settled for liberal use of skin glue, steri-strips and a well-wrapped bandage. I tried to get my fingers beneath that bandage to get at the maddening itch while we waited.

To take my mind off that particular discomfort, I shifted to ease the stiffness in my legs from crouching against the garage in the alley behind the stash house. With the information from Zak Mackey, we had more than enough probable cause, and all three teams that made up our task force had been in position for over an hour. We were just waiting for the search warrant and green light from Captain Curran, who was coordinating the raid from an unmarked van down the block.

"Doin' okay, Luck?"

I tore my gaze from the eerily quiet house. Ray was so shabbily dressed today he looked more like he should be frequenting the house than busting it. "Yeah, I'm cool."

"Curran must have been pissed about all that paperwork, huh."

"What paperwork?"

He gestured to my arm. "Gettin' hurt in the line and all. Those reports are a bitch."

"Oh, yeah, right." If I had told her she would have no doubt been pissed. She didn't need to know everything.

For something new to fidget with, I pulled the elastic from my ponytail and shook out my long black hair before retying it loosely to give my scalp a break. Everything was getting stiff. I couldn't fathom how Monroe kept her hair so tight all the time. I was still holding out hope for the day when I worked up the nerve to just cut it all off. "Hate this bullshit waiting game. Everything Sky's given us has been good. She knows what's up."

Ray scoffed. "Up her nose, you mean. What even was that the other day? Bath salts? Fuckin' scary."

He wasn't wrong, and I couldn't defend her on that one, so I ignored the comment. "The longer this takes the more likely she is to get made."

"Yeah, well, we blow in there too early and anything we find is inadmissible."

"I know the law, Ray. I promised her after this I'd cut her loose and get her record cleared. I'm gonna help her find her sister, get set up somewhere new, and get back on her feet. She's just a kid."

"She's twenty and she attacked you. She's a user and a criminal with a record as long as my di—"

"Gimme a break, Ray. You know what she's been through. She's a warrior."

He sighed quietly. "She's not you, Lucky. She may not be able to turn it around."

"She deserves a chance." I returned my gaze to the house.

A moment later a low buzz sounded, pulling my attention from the house again. "That's you, pal."

"What? Oh. Jesus, you got like bionic hearing." He pulled his phone from beneath his Kevlar vest. "It's the captain."

"Better not be a problem with the warrant," I muttered.

"Yeah, boss." He listened intently, his brows knitting together. "What? Yeah, send it to me."

"What's up?"

"An OUT analyst received a video. She's sending it through."

"What now?" The Online Undercover Tips site was a new initiative to combat crime in near real time. With nearly everyone with smartphone video capability and the gleeful willingness to record suspicious people or crimes in progress, you could now upload the information directly to the police. It worked like walking citywide CCTV footage. A room full of tech nerds vetted it, cleaned it up, and passed it along to the appropriate department.

"Oh, fuck," he hissed.

"What?" I leaned over his shoulder to see the video clip taken at the back door of the very house we were watching. Sky, head lolling and bare feet dragging, was being helped up the back walkway by a large, bald, tattooed man I wasn't familiar with. "Jesus, she can't even walk. What the fuck did they do to her? When was this? What team was on watch?"

"Captain said it just came through, but the time stamp has been scrubbed. The techs are still working on it."

"Son of a bitch!" I surged to my feet and my sidearm was in my hand before I registered pulling it.

Ray's hand was on my arm. "You can't. There's no warrant yet."

"There's probable cause."

"We don't know she's in there."

"I'm going, Ray."

I stayed low to make myself a smaller target for anyone in the house who could be looking to fire on me from any of the many windows on this side of the house. The sound of Ray moving behind me was drowned out by the crackling of my earpiece comms coming to life.

"Team three, hold your position." Captain Curran's voice sounded so loud it was like she was standing right next to me.

I kept moving, tucking up against the house to the side of the back door with Ray on the other side looking panicked and uncertain. I didn't have time to worry about the consequences of my actions.

"Sorin, Keller, return to your position. That is an order." Angela's voice was strained in an effort not to yell. I knew that voice all too well.

Be cool. Be cool. The door handle turned easily. It was open. I locked eyes with Ray, who was shaking his head frantically.

"The hell you think you're doing, Sorin?" Monroe hissed over comms.

"What is going on?" Lyons muttered through the earpiece. "Captain, please advise."

"Sorin, goddamn it, stand down!" Angela finally roared in my ear.

I pulled the earpiece and let it hang before holding up my hand, counting down from three.

Ray's glare was hateful, but he'd have my back. I whipped the door open and stepped in, elbows tucked in and my Glock 19 close to my body. Heart drumming against my rib cage, my breathing deep and even. Sweat trickled down my temple. No more time to think about it.

Ray's hand on my shoulder let me know he was behind me and we moved through the kitchen as one. It was spotless. The empty cabinets stood open and the smell of bleach hung in the air. The wood floors in the dining room were battered but so clean they squeaked—same with the walls. The house had been scrubbed.

We moved through the house wordlessly, clearing each room—kitchen, dining, living and two bedrooms. It didn't take long. The bathroom door was ajar and I glanced at Ray who gave me a quick nod. I opened the door and sucked in a sharp breath.

I could smell her before I saw her. The stench of unwashed body and illness. Sky was in the bathtub fully clothed—the same tattered clothes she was wearing when I saw her last. One filthy, colorless arm dangled over the side and her legs splayed out, the bare soles of her feet black. Her head tilted to rest on her shoulder, her filmy eyes partially open and frothy blood staining her chin and shirt.

"Fuck, no, Sky." I holstered my weapon and dropped to my knees beside her. "No. No. No. No. Help me, Ray." I tried to get a grip around her and get her out, but her lifeless body just slipped limply through my arms and settled back in the tub.

Ray's hand came down on my shoulder. "Lucky, she's gone."

"No." I sat back on my heels, the hot sting of tears threatening behind my eyes, and my throat tightened painfully. "No. No. I promised her." I stared at her bony chest, willing it to move with an intake of breath. There was nothing. Nothing. Nothing there at all. "Her necklace. Where's her necklace?"

Booted feet thundered through the house now and voices of my team clearing the house again bounced off the barren walls.

"Keller. Sorin. Report."

"Her necklace is missing," I mumbled, staring at nothing.

"Lucy," Angela said, sharply.

I raised my gaze to Captain Curran who filled the narrow doorway. Even in a place as bleak as a dingy bathroom in a drug den, Angela Curran elevated the moment with her poised confidence. The woman who had saved my life, taken me under her wing, and who I considered a mentor and a friend, looked anything but that at the moment. Her gaze was steel as she took in the scene.

"It's Skyler Kingston," I said, uncertain if I was going to be able to move from the spot on the floor as the adrenaline leached out of me and grief and rage filled in the spaces.

Captain Curran's expression flashed with compassion for a moment before hardening again and flicking to Keller. "Get her out of here."

I was too numb to do anything but let Ray help me to my feet and lead me out of the house to the sound of the captain demanding our report be completed by the time she got back to the station.

Captain Curran did not hold back. "You two violated a direct order and wasted a judge's time, not to mention my time and the rest of your team. You have so thoroughly botched this operation you brought the mayor down on the chief and the chief down on me."

I tried not to fidget as Ray and I stood at attention. I was in deep shit and I hadn't even been able to save Sky. As long as the captain focused her ire on me I could avoid thinking about Sky and what working for me had cost her. At the very least, I could avoid taking Ray down with me. "It was all me. Ray didn't—"

"Didn't stop you," Ray cut me off, always having my back.

"Save it," Curran said, tapping her pen against her desk. "This task force, of which you two are the most *junior* members, has put in countless hours to find the locations of the Rat Lords MC stash houses and in one afternoon, because of your reckless insubordination, we are set back to square one."

My jaw clenched and I shook my head.

"Something to say, Sorin?"

"We've logged the hours, too."

The captain arched a brow. "Would you care to take that up with Forbes and Monroe? This bust was theirs and I expect you'll be hearing from them before too long."

Fuck them. We'd all put in the same hours and without me, Forbes and Monroe would still be looking for the damn house. I squared my shoulders. "Our going in there before the warrant was issued didn't damage the case. Sky got made somehow and they knew we were coming and cleared everything out. There was nothing useful in there to find."

"You know that for certain, do you? You know that there was nothing for forensics to find? Nothing we could use to build our case but is now inadmissible because of you? Are you certain there was nothing in that house to link that goddamn motorcycle club to the fentanyl-laced cocaine raining down on the city? To the weapons that have popped up in at least three fatal shootings this month? Did you know for certain before charging in there—against direct orders—that there wasn't a scrap of evidence, scuff of soot, or drop of accelerant that would connect them to the fire at Cherry Hill apartments that burned the home of thirty families to the ground, injured dozens, and killed five people—two of them children?"

I winced, unable to hold her glare. My throat tightened and voice cracked. "No, ma'am. I don't know."

"No. You don't."

I had done the right thing. Hadn't I? Sky could've been in trouble. She was in trouble. I just hadn't been in time. "*You* sent us that video. What did you think I was going to do?"

Her voice went cold. "So this is on me?"

"No, ma'am," Ray said before I could dig myself deeper.

"Sky was in trouble and I had a chance to save her."

"She's not in trouble anymore, is she? Your informant. Your responsibility."

I swallowed hard around the tightness in my throat and refused to cry. "She was my friend, Ang."

"Captain Curran," she snapped and stood abruptly. "Detective Keller, you are dismissed."

"Captain, permission to spe—"

"Denied. Get out."

Ray's lips pressed together in a hard line and he shot me a sympathetic look before he hustled out the door, dodging Clay Craig who appeared to be waiting his turn to speak to the captain. I wanted to keep staring at the door he closed behind him to avoid looking back at Angela. I stalled as long as I could before turning my attention back to her. Her expression had softened somewhat and she looked older than I had ever seen her look as she slumped back into her chair.

"I am sorry about Skyler, Lucy."

"Thank you. What about the man she was with? Has he been identified? Maybe we—"

"Not yet. The techs are still going over the video. There's something else we need to discuss. I know this may not seem like the best time, but I'm afraid it might be the only time."

I rubbed my bleary eyes and gestured to the chair in front of me. Angela nodded and I dropped into it like my strings had been cut. "Time for what?"

"To set up your cover."

I gaped at her. And then laughed out loud. A real genuine bark of amusement. "If they know Sky is…*was*…talking to the police then they know about me."

"That wouldn't matter if you were no longer on the job," she said almost inaudibly.

I straightened. "What?"

Angela took a deep breath and placed her hands flat on her desk, as if to steady herself. "This breach in protocol, insubordination, risking your life and your partner's, damaging our case. I can't overlook it, Detective Sorin. There will be formal consequences."

I sighed wearily. "I understand. Like what?"

"The mayor and the chief want someone to answer for this. It will have to be discussed, but no doubt up to and including termination. This city cannot have—and I cannot have—officers on this force who are not up to the job."

I blinked. "What? I'm sorry, what are we talking about here? You're firing me? I thought you just said you were setting up my cover."

"I am," she said pointedly, her expression unreadable.

My head throbbed. "What does that even mean?"

"Listen to me very carefully, Lucy. You don't have to go through with it and even if you choose to, you can come out and come back whenever you want. But if and when you go in, whatever happens after, you'll be on your own. No handler. No contact. No backup. No one can know what you're doing except me. After this conversation we won't speak of this again. Do you understand?"

"What the hell, Ang? You don't need a cop, you need a spy. No, I don't understand."

"You will. I believe in you and I trust you, Lucy. Please, trust me."

CHAPTER FIVE

My one-bedroom apartment was neat. It wasn't hard to keep things tidy when you didn't have much. I had barely enough growing up and it was for that reason alone I could leave home as fast as I had and that had saved my life. There was nothing to worry about going back for. I lived like that still.

The one sofa was comfortable enough and the coffee table solid. I had a laptop and Internet, but no cable. I'd watched enough garbage television in the home to last a lifetime. Anything worth watching I could stream now. The few books lying around were picked up at yard sales for pennies. There was no art on the walls. I had Bluetooth speakers when I wanted music. By the door was my gym bag I used a few times a week. I didn't even have my own membership and went as a guest to Angela's gym and shared her locker. For payment I *let* her kick my ass when we sparred hand-to-hand. There ended the list of my entertainment amenities.

I stripped off my sweater and tossed it directly into the washing machine of the apartment-size stackable unit. I didn't even own a hamper. Clothes went directly into the washer and came out of the dryer when I needed them back on my body. In the bedroom I removed my sidearm, checked the safety, and tucked it into the nightstand. Here sat one of my only personal touches and I picked it up. A small framed photograph of me and Angela in front of a crooked, paint-chipped wooden sign that read "Second Chances," taken a year after I made it to the group home. It was a small summer camp off Seven Lakes Drive about an hour and a half south of Albany. Children's Services ran it and a couple of times a year different group homes got together and held overnight camp for the residents.

I always tried to play it cool when it was camp time. Like it didn't matter to me one way or another, but the smile plastered on my face gave me away every time. I loved camp and I loved getting to share it with Angela whenever she was able to get away and come for a visit. I bet Sky had never been to camp. The camp had long since been cut from Children's Services' budget and the property long abandoned, though I knew it all still physically existed. I drove down there once and wandered around the old buildings at the suggestion of my therapist to make peace with my past. I set the picture back in its place and headed for the kitchen.

The unused appliances gleamed and the fridge held only enough food to keep me alive. There had never been any family to visit me and there were no dates to impress with snacks or culinary skills.

Not that I couldn't have used a good fuck right about now. I only ever went home with women when the need arose and always to their place. That way I could leave whenever I wanted, which was usually pretty quick. No one had ever been in here but Angela. Ray, only ever as far as the door when we were going out. Angela understood why I felt the need to live like this despite her occasional efforts trying to set me up with someone. It wasn't that I wasn't capable of having more in my life—more things or more people. I was. I am. I'm not so damaged that I'm unable to form attachments. It just never works out in my favor, so I've quit trying. For me there is safety in remaining unattached. To things and to people. Sky was an exception.

There had been a woman from the academy. Rebecca Hart. She was funny and smart and she genuinely enjoyed me. I enjoyed her, too, and we even got as far as calling ourselves girlfriends for the better part of a year. She told me she loved me many times and I was thinking about returning the sentiment. I wasn't sure if it was true, but it certainly felt the closest I'd ever been to being in love. I told her things about me no one else knew and she listened without judgment and stayed without expectation. It was the first time I wanted to hold on to someone.

She was killed in a crash while making a traffic stop. A pimply-faced kid answering a text slammed into her cruiser from behind, crushing her between her cruiser and the stopped car. She hadn't died right away, lingering in the ICU long enough for me to meet her parents and younger brothers who'd flown in from Colorado. They were lovely and accepting and welcoming. They asked me to stand with them by her bedside when they turned off the machines. I still get Christmas cards but haven't spoken to them since the funeral.

I pulled down the nearly empty bottle of Johnnie Walker Black and poured what was left into one of the three glasses I owned. There was an unopened bottle behind it. I tossed back the two fingers in one swallow and breathed in while it burned down my throat. Even if Angela hadn't been supportive of my going into law enforcement, I'm sure I would have found my way there eventually. V.I. Warshawski was my hero from the moment I first picked up the battered copy of *Blood Shot* at the group home. I read as many of Sara Paretsky's novels as I could get my hands on. Nancy Drew was for the good girls with loving families and friends. I needed a girl from the mean streets solving crime with grit and smarts. Making a name for herself with a Smith and Wesson in one hand and a bottle of Black Label in the other and not taking shit from anyone along the way. That was me.

Yeah, right. I'm so tough.

Even one drink loosened the grip I had over my emotions. Instead of crying over Sky into the fresh bottle and continuing to puzzle over Angela's cryptic words, I gave my pits a quick swipe of Mountain Sport and headed out.

I held the busted rack together at Copper Jacks and carefully eased the triangle off the tightly racked balls. I used it enough and could make it work for me. I didn't bother with my cue tonight and I had no interest in a proper match of nine-ball, so bar pool eight-ball would do.

I'd been running the table for an hour and there were four quarters lined up along the rail, marking how many challengers were waiting their turn. Most cops didn't bother playing me anymore to avoid a bruised ego, preferring to wait for one of the other tables to open. The ones that did put a quarter up were just looking for a good-natured game playing for drinks, of which I'd already won more than my fair share.

My opponent now was a young college guy with a group of friends hoping to take over the table so they could play doubles. I let him break and he sank the two and twelve. I leaned against the wall with my favorite house cue in one hand and a beer in the other, watching him circle the table like he knew what he was doing. It was a good break and if he had any skill at all, he could probably run out, but I suspected he was all flash and no finesse.

"Figured I'd find you here," Ray said as he came up behind me and placed a fresh beer for me on the high-top table nearby. "What are you playing?"

"He dropped one of each on the break."

"This kid any good?" he asked as the kid in question leaned across the table. His left hand formed a loose, closed bridge and his right jerked the shaft back and forth like he was going for another break. He banged the cue ball scattering the already open table even more and dropping another solid.

"Nope." I grabbed up the chalk and stepped toward the table, but the kid lined up another shot.

"I got one in," he said.

"You didn't call it."

"So? Take a seat, honey. I'll let you know when it's your turn." His friends guffawed from their table.

Ray's mouth dropped comically and he looked back and forth from the kid to me. "You gonna let him get away with that?"

I shrugged and returned to my spot against the wall, taking a long swallow of the fresh beer. "Doesn't matter to me."

Ray was quiet a long moment. "You doin' okay? About Sky?"

The bands of grief tightened around my chest at the mention of her name. I drew in a long breath to loosen them and closed my eyes until the threat of tears passed. And then lied. "I'm okay."

"Did Curran hand you our ass?"

Among other things. "I'm on probation. Maybe more."

"You were already on probation for wrecking the car."

"Well, now it's double secret probation, I guess." It was so hard not to talk to Ray about all the other stuff. How did Angela think I was going to go undercover without him knowing?

He barked a laugh. "I'm so sorry I ever introduced you to *Animal House*."

"So am I."

"The techs showed me the cleaned-up stills of the video. The guy with Sky has a Rat Lords tattoo. Still no ID on him, though."

"Yeah, I figured."

"We'll know for sure after the autopsy, but everything points to an overdose."

My jaw clenched. "She was careful. She wanted out. The Rat Lords did this to her."

"That's going to be tough to prove."

"Whose fucking side are you on, Ray?"

"Sorry, I just—"

"Forget it. It's cool."

He leaned in, bumping my shoulder with his. "What a stupid fucking name, anyway. Rat Lords. Why not kings? That's a thing, right? Rat kings?"

I snorted. "You know what a rat king is?"

"Do you?"

"It's like this cluster of rats knotted together by their tails with sap or grease and they just get stuck like that and die eating each other because they can't agree which way to go."

"Nasty."

It was. And so were they. I shook my head fiercely. "I'm not letting her go out like that, Ray."

"What does that mean? What are you gonna do?"

What was I going to do? Not much if I got myself fired. "I don't know, but someone is going to answer for her death."

"You're up, sexy!" the kid hollered, and leered at me from where he leaned back against his table, thrusting his pelvis in my general direction and making a show of ogling me.

His antics caught me a little off-guard. Just about everyone else here knew which end of the Kinsey scale I was on. I knew the kid's bullshit didn't actually mean he found me attractive. It was just a power move. And a trash one at that. I wasn't curvy or slender, but somewhere in between. What did that make me? Pretty average, I guess, at five foot seven and one sixty-five. I did okay with the ladies probably because of the handcuffs and tight T-shirt. No one was going to be bouncing quarters off my abs, but regular workouts kept the jiggle in my arms down and my muffin top under control. My tits weren't world class, but they were the same size and I'd never been mistaken for a man. More than one woman had told me I reminded them of Dexter's sister, Deb—except thicker. That probably had everything to do with my penchant for profanity and bad decisions. Could be worse.

"Be back in a few," I said to Ray and chalked my cue again. The kid had managed to bang in all but two of his balls before missing a shot.

"Excuse me." My preferred shot took me directly in front of their high-top table and I smiled politely and waited for him to move. He laughed and I could feel his stare when I bent in front of him to line up my shot. I did have a nice ass, of that I was aware. I favored an open bridge and slid the cue over the V between my index finger and thumb a couple of times before striking the cue ball and sending the eleven ball into the left corner pocket, stopping the cue ball to put the thirteen in the side right after.

By the third ball, the smile had been wiped from the kid's reddening face and his friends were mocking him relentlessly. I relaxed into a rhythm and didn't look at him again while I ran out, hearing only the sounds of the cue connecting with the ball and the ball dropping into the pocket. Only the eight ball was left and I chalked up again before lining up the shot.

I eyed the fuming kid over my cue and flashed him a smile and wink as I sent the cue ball into the eight and the eight ball down the table hugging the rail and into the corner pocket.

"Bitch," he growled and dug in his pocket for quarters. "Rematch."

"Fuck off, kid." A deep voice rumbled from behind me before sweeping everyone else's quarters off the rail to use for his own game. "I've got next."

I rolled my eyes and went back to my beer. "Come on, Forbes, it's been a hell of a day. Can you not be a dick for like one night?"

Forbes crossed his meaty, muscled arms and leaned back against the table to glower at me. Beads of sweat dotted his bald brown head. Lyons and Neal strolled up to the other side of the table to watch whatever was about to go down.

Before Forbes had a chance to respond, Monroe stalked over and into my face. I could smell gin on her breath. She was two inches shorter than me and about twenty pounds of muscle heavier. "He wouldn't need to be such a dick if you weren't such a fuck-up, Sorin. You're not the only one on this unit and your bullshit has just added hours and a shit-ton of work for us."

"Us, too, Sorin," Neal chimed in from a safe distance away.

"Shut the hell up, Neal." Ray jabbed a finger in his direction. "Back off, Monroe. No one asked you."

Monroe's gaze flicked to him. "You better cut your losses, Keller, or you're going down with her. Maybe you can sit bitch on patrol with Lyons and Neal."

"Fuck that," Neal sneered, clearly not getting that was just as much a dig at him as Ray.

"I'll take my chances," Ray said.

I shot him an appreciative glance at his willingness to stick by me.

"Well, I won't," Monroe snarled. "Maybe now that your useless little side piece is out of the game you'll be less likely to jam us up with the shit you pulled today."

"My *what*?" Be cool. Be cool.

"Lucky, take it easy," Ray warned.

"That shit-for-brains excuse for an informant you been working," Forbes said.

My teeth ground painfully. Maybe I was wrong about not forming attachments to people. I sure felt pretty attached to Sky right now. And I sure as hell wasn't going to let these assholes talk shit about her. "If it weren't for her we wouldn't have had the location of that house."

Forbes scoffed. "If it weren't for her getting made, we might actually have a case against the Lords, right now."

"Fuck you, Forbes. An innocent girl is dead."

He straightened off the table to his full six-foot-three height and towered over me. "That's 'fuck you, *Sergeant* Forbes'. And maybe if she'd paid more attention to where she was going and less to going down on you, she'd still be—"

His head snapped back when my fist connected solidly with his mouth, splitting my knuckles on his teeth. I didn't have time to worry about my hand when powerful arms wrapped around me from behind, pinning my arms to my sides.

Ray shouted and started toward us, but not before Monroe lifted me off my feet and threw me down onto my side in a crushing body slam.

The groan from the air whooshing from my lungs sounded inhuman and pain rattled through my entire skeleton. "Ah, fuck…"

"You're finished, Sorin." Forbes spat a wad of blood from his split and swelling mouth onto the floor by my head. "Good luck in the motor pool."

CHAPTER SIX

"You wanted to see me, Captain?" I stood in the doorway of Angela's office first thing in the morning, waiting for an invitation to enter this time. My head pounded, my hand throbbed, and my heart ached.

"*Want* to see you, Sorin? No." She turned from her office window overlooking the parking lot, her face an unreadable mask. "But I did *ask* to see you. Come in."

I moved into the room and started to close the door.

"Leave it open."

"Ma'am?"

"The walls have ears." She paused for a beat and fixed her gaze on mine. "And I don't want anyone to misconstrue what's going on here. It will serve us both in the long run if everyone simply hears firsthand. I don't want our personal relationship to be used against either one of us should you choose to appeal my decision."

"Appeal what decision?" My heart sped up and I kept my trembling hands clasped tightly behind my back.

"You're entitled to have a union representative if you choose," she said.

"I don't understand. What's going on?"

"Sergeant Forbes filed a formal complaint with Human Resources, the union, and the chief. Conduct unbecoming an officer, insubordination, and assault of a senior officer."

I flexed my sore and swollen right hand, unable to hide a slightly satisfied curl of my lip at smacking the smug grin off that motherfucker. "I see."

"I don't think you do. You've put me in an impossible situation and I have no choice but to remove you from Street Crimes effective immediately."

"What? No way I'm riding a desk."

"No. You're to get into uniform and report to the desk sergeant over at—"

"Patrol? Angela, come on. I busted my ass to make detective, you know that. You can't do that."

"I can and I did. I'm sorry, Lucy."

"You didn't back me up with the chief? What about what we just talked about? What about—"

"All I've done since you started with this unit is back you up, but you make it so damn hard. You're so smart, you've got great instincts, and you have so much empathy for those you serve. Maybe too much. You can't take everything so personally if you're going to survive doing this work. Lucy, you are an excellent cop, and if you can get your head on straight I see amazing things for you."

"But?" I said, my voice strained even to my own ears.

"But maybe moving up to detective was too soon. I pushed you and you weren't ready and that's on me."

"I *was* ready. I aced that exam. I've got this."

"It's not about your test score. I thought you were ready, too, but now with Skyler Kingston's death...you got too close, too involved."

"No goddamn it! You can't take me off this case. I promised her."

"Lower your voice and listen to what I'm saying, Officer Sorin," she barked.

"*Officer*? So it's like that, huh, Ang?"

She pinned me with a hard-eye stare I knew all too well and I clamped down on my next words. "As I was saying, you are to report to Sergeant Fonseca at Center Station for your assignment."

Be cool. Be cool. I sucked in a sharp breath and returned the captain's stare pound for pound. This is what she meant, right? This was my cover. Right? Or did I really just get demoted? Oh, Jesus. There was no going back now. "No."

Her eyes narrowed, her nod almost imperceptible. "This isn't forever, Lucy, but it's not up for discussion. The decision, however, is yours. Take the demotion, toe the line, and restore this department's trust in you."

I was right. Wasn't I? I needed to think but I had no time. Our last few conversations going back to the last time I saw Sky alive swirled through my mind. I tried desperately to grasp hold of all the pieces, but they floated just out of reach. "Or what?"

Expressions flitted across her face too fast and too many to name—worry, fear, and was that…pride? "Or you do what you have to do," she said finally, her mouth settling into a grim line, and her gaze unwavering.

I nodded and my hands visibly trembled as I unclipped my gold shield from my belt. I ran my thumb over the shining metal before tossing it onto her desk in dramatic fashion like I'd seen done in countless television shows. It bounced facedown.

She stared at it for a long time, the silence hanging heavy in the air between us. "You understand what this means?"

"Yes." It came out barely a whisper. Did I? Hell no, but I was getting more confident in my decision with each passing second.

She inhaled deeply and nodded, giving me yet another opportunity to back out and take my demotion. "Are you sure this is what you want, Lucy?"

"Yes." This time with more conviction.

"I'll need your service weapon."

My hands didn't shake this time when I pulled the holster from my belt and handed over my sidearm still strapped in.

Angela released the safety strap and pulled my weapon, ensuring the chamber was clear and releasing the magazine. She spent a long moment moving my shield and sidearm into a drawer in her desk before handing me back my holster. "I don't need this."

I squeezed it, intending to hurl it across the room in a very real fit of frustrated rage when I noticed the scrap of paper in it. I froze for a moment then clipped it back onto my belt.

"Please, take care, Lucy," Angela said softly.

I gave her a sharp nod. "Thanks for everything, Ang. I'll see ya around."

It was unnaturally quiet when I emerged from Captain Curran's office. No phones ringing, no keyboards clicking, no loud conversations or chairs scraping. All eyes were on me and no one in the department even bothered to pretend they hadn't heard what had happened, as much as they could anyway from wherever their desk was situated.

Lyons and Neal, who should have been out on patrol by now, were hanging by the coffeemaker with Clay Craig. They turned away as soon as I looked over at them. Cowards. Clay stared at me, his mustache giving away nothing.

Forbes and Monroe leaned against *my* desk which was close enough to Angela's office to hear everything. They straightened up and crossed their arms in unison, wearing matching triumphant smirks. They were likely hoping I needed to go through them to get my personal items from my desk. I didn't have any. Suck it, assholes.

Ray looked pitiful as he stood, rocking from foot to foot, his hands in and out of his pockets. He was even scruffier than usual—like a beaten dog at the pound—guilty for something he hadn't even done. I couldn't look at him. There was nothing I could say to help him understand, so I walked right by and out the doors.

"Lucky, wait!"

I knew he would follow, but I didn't slow. I just needed to get home and think and figure out what my next move was going to be.

"Wait, goddamn it!" His hand gripped my arm and pulled me to a stop in front of the building.

"Get off, Ray." I jerked my arm free.

"What's going on? You turned in your shield? What the hell?"

I shrugged. "Seemed like a good idea at the time."

"What are you talking about? Take patrol for six months and then come back. Or, go to the union and appeal Curran's decision."

"It's done." I started walking again. I couldn't stand to see the hurt look of betrayal on his face. No attachments? Yeah, right. Who the hell was I kidding? I loved Ray and he deserved better.

"What about me? I'm your partner. This really how you're gonna do me, Lucky?"

Grief washed over me again and I fought against tears to keep my voice steady. I kept walking and called over my shoulder, "Go home, Ray. Or…go to work, I guess."

He didn't respond and didn't come after me, but I could feel his eyes on me as I paused at the entrance to the parking lot. It wasn't my car and I didn't need anything out of it, so I dug the keys from my pocket and hurled them in the general direction of all the identical unmarked cars and kept walking.

My day so far had been absolute shit and it was only nine in the morning. I hadn't felt this badly about myself, or felt so alone, since I first left home. I had no problem cracking open that fresh bottle of Black Label and pouring myself an enormous morning drink. V.I. sure as shit would have.

My empty—but not entirely empty—holster sat on my coffee table next to the bottle while I sucked on my cheap scotch. I needed answers but had never been more terrified to get them. Turning in my badge didn't mean I had to do anything. It just meant I quit my job. It didn't commit me to a dangerous course of undercover work with no backup and no one but Angela Curran knowing what I was up to. Somehow, though, I knew if I looked at the scrap of paper Angela had slipped me, there would be no turning back.

I replayed our conversations in our head. She hadn't ever discussed an undercover assignment with me in front of anyone else. She was vague and noncommittal about the details. Except that I'd have no support. Did the chief even know? He must. She made sure to tell me in not so many words that she was being watched. She gave me a clear choice and told me as much as she could. She trusted me to put the pieces together and needed it all to happen loudly and publicly to set my cover.

The proverbial penny dropped. Holy shit! She thought there was a mole in the department. Someone in the department was on the Rat Lords' payroll. It's the only thing that made sense. Why else would Angela By-the-Book Curran be so cagey?

I had to roll it around in my head a couple of different ways before the answer hit home—square in the chest, sucking the air from my lungs. Sky didn't get made. Someone ratted her out. One of us? One of the team? Oh, shit. Oh, shit. Sky, I'm so sorry.

I slugged my drink and nearly gagged it back up before slamming down the glass and snatching up the holster. My decision had been made and I was all in. I turned the holster upside down and a square of paper fluttered onto the table, word side up. I didn't touch it.

Hit the gym and work it out

My gym bag was still next to the front door. It was flat, the clothes and towels having settled from disuse over the last few days. I couldn't remember when I was there last. Probably before we started round-the-clock surveillance on the stash house. Angela and I used the same gym.

I snatched up the bag and looked for my car keys. Oh, right. I had no idea what the bus schedule looked like. Guess I was hoofin' it until I found out. Welcome to your new life, Sorin.

The gym was fairly quiet at eleven in the morning on a random Tuesday. It took me nearly an hour to run-walk the three miles to the gym from my place, including the time to stop and puke up my early morning drink behind a dumpster.

Be cool. Be cool. I lingered over the water fountain. Was I being watched? Everyone knew by now I'd been fired. Or quit. Whatever. Why would they be watching me? To see if I retaliated for Sky's death? If the Rat Lords knew Sky was an informant, they knew I was her handler. Why was I still alive? Because I wasn't a threat. That stung a little. Because they knew she hadn't told us anything they couldn't cover their tracks on. They were still in the clear. Sky was dead and I was off the job.

I worked my way through my usual sets for arm-and-shoulder day before heading to the women's locker room. I had to wash my hands for a really long time until the room cleared and I could retrieve my key card from between the sink mirror and the wall where I kept it stashed. One less thing for me to keep track of.

Angela paid for a full-size locker for both of us. It was exactly as I expected it to look. She kept spare office clothes hung neatly. I kept my emergency set of work clothes ranger-rolled atop an old pair of boots on the bottom. Toiletries, towel, and a couple of protein bars were on the top shelf. I munched on one while I pushed the clothes around to see if there was... Jackpot!

A small plastic baggie was wrapped in my T-shirt. I stuffed it down my pants until I got into a bathroom stall. I kicked the seat down and sat before unwrapping it. There was a small black burner phone and I powered it on. The screen blinked with a single text message from a number I didn't recognize.

Call this number when you're ready to come out

I powered the phone back off and dropped it back in the plastic bag. There were four glossy three-by-five still photos from the video of Sky being taken into the stash house, seemingly zooming in on the back of her head. The enhanced photo of the back of the biker's head showed a fuzzy tattoo I recognized as a Nazi symbol adopted by white supremacist groups. The photos were increasingly enlarged until I could barely tell what I was looking at. I didn't understand and started over from the beginning.

I let my eyes relax. If the people were out of focus, what was in focus? The house. The windows. The reflections in the windows. Oh shit. Whoever took that video was clever enough to make sure they weren't reflected in the shot, but what was that? A reflection of the front of a car parked in the alleyway? A nondescript, black four-door sedan with a bull bar—police issue.

The pictures dropped from my shaking hands and I quickly scooped them up. Another woman had come into the locker room. My heart hammered in my chest while I shredded the pictures into small pieces. I had to flush three times to get them to clear the bowl.

"You all right?" the woman asked when I finally emerged from the stall.

I forced a smile and patted my belly. "Two coffees and a bran muffin."

She grunted. "Heard that."

I stuffed the phone back into the locker. I couldn't keep it on me and I couldn't take it home. Here was as good a place as any. It wasn't open twenty-four hours, but it would have to do. It was time to get to work.

First order of business was to run back home, without puking.

CHAPTER SEVEN

I banked the cue off one rail and drilled the nine into the side to end the last game. I straightened and blew the errant lock of hair out of my face. As much as I loved my new choppy, layered short hair, it came with a drawback, the longer layers sometimes fell into my eyes when I leaned over. I was getting used to it and it hadn't stopped me from winning a race to seven games against the reddening and sweating forty-something businessman across the table.

He had long since tossed his jacket aside. By the third game he ripped off his already loosened tie and rolled up his sleeves. When I put him out of his misery, without allowing him even a turn at the table for the last game, I imagined I could hear his panicked heart beating wildly in his chest. He snatched up his jacket and cue and bolted.

I picked up the thick stack of bills from the table where it had sat for the last two hours. It had steadily grown from two hundred to eight hundred dollars while I slowly worked him over. I let him win more than I beat him for an hour and waited patiently while he went to the ATM down the block—twice—to keep sweetening the pot. He was surely thinking by the end of the night he was going to be surprising his wife with a weekend away. Now, he was heading home to explain why they couldn't make a car payment this month.

I jammed the cash in my pocket and rested my AF8 bird's-eye maple cue on the table, never leaning it against the wall, to prevent it from warping.

"Hey, Lucky."

I froze at the sound of Ray's voice behind me and didn't turn around. "You shouldn't be here, Ray."

"Neither should you. Do you have any idea how long I've been looking for you?"

I turned. "Three months or so? I'm not really keeping track."

He blinked. "Your hair. It's…You look different."

I ran a hand through it, shaking up the layers. I'd traded in the pressed chinos and V-neck sweaters for a new uniform of black jeans and fitted short-sleeve button downs with the sleeves rolled and buttons strategically undone to flash glimpses down my shirt when I played. I'd gone full dyke but was still prepared to use cleavage to my advantage with the boys. "What are you doing here, Ray?"

"Looking for you, what the hell do you think? You haven't returned my calls, you're never at your apartment. Hell, the only reason I knew you weren't fucking dead is that I'm your emergency contact, so someone would've called me."

I took a long swallow from my beer. "How did you find me?"

"Jesus, really? How about, 'Hey, Ray, how've you been? Sorry, I flushed my career down the shitter leaving you hanging, and then dropped off the face of the fucking earth. And then made you come looking for me at the ass end of the shittiest dive bar in the city.' What the actual fuck are you doing at Chumps?"

He wasn't wrong. It was an absolute hole. One you had to actually take a flight of steps down to get in. There were no windows and the place was lit with bare swinging bulbs. What little furniture it had looked like it had been blindly selected from restaurant castoffs. Nothing matched or was even entirely intact. The floor was always sticky and damp as were most of the patrons. "I'm working."

"Working?"

I pulled the wad of cash from my pocket and flashed it at him. "Two hours and I made more cash than I brought home in two days with the badge."

"Jesus Christ."

"Check this out." I peeled off a five-dollar bill and held it up. Someone had doodled in black ink all over Lincoln's hair and ears and written the words, *Live long and prosper*. "I got a Spocked fiver."

Before he could say more, a door banged open behind the bar and a woman walked out in heels so high and a black minidress so tight she shouldn't have been able to breathe let alone walk. Nevertheless, she glided out from behind the bar, turning every greasy, gap-toothed head in the place, and stopped at the Coors Light bar mirror to look herself over. She fluffed her long, wavy dark hair and ran a manicured nail carefully beneath a blue eye to fix a smudge of eyeliner. She plumped her already well-displayed breasts so they nearly spilled out the top of her dress.

This wasn't the first time I had seen her, and every time I did my body went to war with itself at the sight of her. She exuded sex and danger and my sensible law enforcement-trained mind told me to stay far away. My traitorous body, on the other hand, shivered with longing to have those breasts filling my hands and my mouth, and have that woman run her nails across my naked skin—and be very careful with them in other places.

The door behind the bar opened again and out strode another woman I could only describe as wicked-looking. She wore full leathers, had tightly-braided hair and dead eyes. Like if Maleficent and Wednesday Addams had a daughter, except sluttier and more muscular. She pressed up against the woman in the dress, grabbing her ass hard enough to make her flinch and whispering something in her ear gross enough to make her visibly shudder.

I'd never seen her before and if there was such a thing as hate at first sight, this was it. Her eyes flicked to me, her lip curling, suggesting she felt the same. She flashed the bartender the hand sign of the Rat Lords—crossed first and second finger like an ASL letter R with thumb out making an L and pointed like a gun. As far as gang signs went, I hated to admit, it was really quite clever.

The woman in the dress must have felt the heat of my stare and met my gaze through the reflection in the mirror. Whatever discomfort she had felt at the other woman's touch, she hid well or had moved on from. She touched up bright red lipstick to her full lips, before kissing the mirror right over my reflection. She flashed a teasing smile and strolled out without ever looking behind her and the rest of my grimy world snapped back into focus.

"What the fuck was that?" Ray said.

"What?" I feigned indifference and went back to my beer.

"Do you even know where you are?"

"Chumps. We covered that already."

"This is a Rat Lords bar, Lucky. They're running guns through here."

"So what? This is a decent table and a sucker walks in every other minute and I am flush. I'm not on the case anymore. Hell, I'm not even a cop."

"Do you want to know about Sky?"

I swallowed hard but managed a casual shrug. "She's dead. What's to know?"

"It was fentanyl-laced coke."

"That's not news."

"There was a funeral. Sort of. No one claimed her body. I thought…I thought maybe you would, but you never returned my calls. So, I did. I signed for her and had her cremated and…"

Oh, god. Ray, just stop, please. "Yeah, sorry, um, thanks for doing that."

He sighed heavily, clearly expecting more and certainly deserving it. "Well, whatever. We got an ID on the club member walking her into the house." He pulled his phone and swiped it on. "Look. He one of your new buddies now?"

I stared at the digital mugshot image. Arvin Dell. Six-foot-four, thirty-eight years old, multiple arrests for assault. His head was shaved and his long beard was braided. Fucking Viking-looking piece of shit. "Never seen him. Don't know him." But I will.

"He has the Nazi symbol…what's it called…Odal rune…tattooed on the back of his head." Ray put his phone away.

"I know."

Ray's head cocked. "How?"

The pictures Angela provided and I flushed down the toilet like top-secret government documents. Shit. "Don't they all?"

His eyes narrowed. "He's bad news, Lucky. Real bad news."

"Noted."

I finished my beer. I needed him to leave. If he stayed any longer I'd burst into tears and tell him everything. I missed the hell out of him. I missed Angela. I missed my team, hell I maybe even missed Forbes and Monroe. Nah. But the last few months had been hell.

It wasn't about building a cover; it was about becoming a new person. Someone who slept until the afternoon and stayed out until dawn, drank too much and puked in alleys. I was the woman who fucked in bathroom stalls and hustled games in the sleaziest bars all over the city. If anyone was watching—and I'm certain they were—they were getting a show. "That all?"

Ray scrubbed both his hands over his stubbled face before running them through lank, unkempt hair. At least he fit in. "I found you because we've had this place under surveillance. We're about to raid it and turn it inside out."

"Don't let me stop you." I picked up my cue and unscrewed the shaft from the butt, sliding the two pieces back into the black leather case I wore slung across my back like some dirtbag Xena. I have many skills.

"Did you hear what I just said? We're busting the place. Anyone in here is going to jail."

"You mean now? I better get another beer then."

"Fine. You know what? Fuck you." He headed for the door. "And take me off your emergency contact list. I don't want to know when you get yourself killed."

"Another beer, Tommy." I eased myself onto a rusted barstool covered in splitting brown vinyl. The bar was the only clean surface in the place and attended to by the manager, Tommy Pringle, who wiped at it constantly from behind the bar. He was pushing fifty easy, with thinning, gray hair, full gray beard and belly straining at his belt. He had a quick smile and was happy to let me run the only table whenever I wanted.

He slid a beer in front of me. "Friend of yours?"

"In another life." I took a long pull of my beer. "Hey, that woman that came through a few minutes ago. I've seen her around a few times. Who is she?"

"Which one, sexy or scary?"

My laugh was genuine. "Sexy. I'm not *that* kinky."

"Mira." Tommy grunted. "Mark my words, kid, you don't want any part of that. Mira Allen is Griffin's old lady."

"Griffin the Rat Lord's president? Shit, no way."

A bushy brow twitched at me. "Yes way, so you better put your eyes back in your pants."

"I can't believe she's locked down with him."

"It's not exclusive."

Huh, interesting. "What does that mean?"

"She's a *friend* to a few of the officers. She has a mutually beneficial arrangement with the club, if you know what I mean."

I did. Sort of. I hid my distaste behind another pull of beer. "Not you?"

"Nah. I don't rank that high."

"And the mistress of the dark with her?" I asked casually.

Tommy didn't laugh. "That's the club enforcer, Shade."

The darkness in his expression actually chilled me, but I forced a smile. "You say that like you're invoking a demon."

The muscles in his jaw bunched. "Way worse than that."

There were some serious gaps in our club intel. We were supposed to have profiles on all the officers, but I'd never heard her mentioned. Did she get missed or did someone on the inside keep her off our radar intentionally? My phone pinged a text message and I gave it a glance, grateful to have somewhere else to look. It was Ray and I read his text for the first time in months.

Last chance

I exhaled a long breath and lifted my cue case off my shoulder, resting it carefully on the bar. I didn't want it to get broken or mistaken for a weapon. I had an opportunity here to make a play. "You know I used to be a cop, right?"

"Sure, Lucky. Everyone knows that."

"Do you trust me, Tommy?"

He barked a laugh. "Hell, no. But I like you just the same. You got grit, kid. Which is why when you started comin' 'round I cleared it with Griff. You get to stay 'cause he allows it, but I gotta keep an eye on you."

"Keep your enemies close, huh?"

"Somethin' like that."

I nodded and sipped my beer. I could work with this. "Would you believe me if I told you the cops are about to light this place up and you've got about one minute to clear out anything the club won't be able to get out from under?"

He gaped at me. "What?"

"Fifty seconds, now. Maybe less."

"Fuck." The glass he was holding hit the floor and shattered. He bolted through the door behind the bar.

It was closer to two minutes and gave me enough time to finish my beer before the door crashed off its hinges. I leapt off my stool in time to see a flash grenade sail through the door. Oh, hell. I was not ready for that.

The explosive concussion of light and sound blew the guys next to me right off their stools and rocked me back into the bar and then down onto my knees. I covered my ears which felt like they had ruptured. Smoke filled my lungs and tears streamed down my face from the visual assault. I couldn't hear anything but painful ringing and could only see dark shadows of legs as they ran back and forth in front of me.

A pair of booted feet stopped in front of me and I blinked into the haze, in time to see an enormous figure in SWAT gear raise the butt of his rifle. Pain exploded in my head and I lost command of my body and crumpled onto my side.

CHAPTER EIGHT

"Get up, Sorin."

I rolled over on the narrow bench I'd been sleeping on during my seventy-two-hour stay in holding. It was the longest they could keep me without charges. I'd been alone for most of the time, but occasionally other women would join me for a few hours at a time. One of them had a pocket full of napkins she offered to me to clean the blood off my face and out of my hair.

After I'd been cuffed and stuffed, the arresting officers covered their asses by getting a paramedic to take a look at me in the back of the patrol car. I had a raging headache and a goose egg on my temple with a small laceration, but I never lost consciousness and didn't need sutures. They weren't really planning on encouraging me to sleep anyway, so there was no chance of my slipping into a coma. I was fit enough to be processed.

No one paid much attention to me, but when the shift changed, new officers would come through to gawk at the disgraced detective and personal friend of Captain Curran who had gotten caught up in the latest Rat Lords raid. The shift changes were how I marked time. They had taken my watch, phone, wallet, and keys along with my bootlaces and belt, lest I try to hang myself. The air was so thick with disdain from my former brothers and sisters in blue, that I got the distinct feeling that given the option, they would have helped me tie the noose.

For the first few hours I honestly thought they'd bounce me out, not wanting me to take up space and resources when they had no reason to hold me and I had been one of them not so long ago. That had been a naive take on the situation, and when the hours turned into days, I knew I was there for the duration. My discomfort and humiliation seemed to be their goal. Though I had committed no crime, apparently blowing that raid and turning in my badge was close enough to crossing the proverbial thin blue line to get me shunned. At least I was in a cell with the toilet on the other side of a low wall for privacy. Small mercies.

No one had come for me—not Angela and not Ray—but late afternoon on day two Forbes and Monroe stopped by with my compartmented serving tray of instant potatoes, lukewarm beans and sausage, canned carrots, one slice of white bread, and a small sour apple.

I picked it up off the floor without comment after Monroe kicked it under the bars, and sat back down on the bench to eat.

"You warned them, didn't you?" she said.

I ignored her and shoveled potatoes into my mouth with the plastic spoon. With a plastic fork I could stab someone, I guess.

"I knew letting Keller go in after you was a mistake but Curran has such a weak spot for you—god help her. You managed to fuck us over again and you're not even on the job," she snarled.

"What do you want, Monroe? You're interrupting my meal."

Forbes came to stand with his partner. "Tell us you tipped them and you'll walk out of here, right now."

"Didn't find what you were looking for, huh? That's a shame."

Her lip curled. "Fuck you."

"You've got nothing to charge me with. I'm gonna walk out of here tomorrow anyway."

"Not if you aided and abetted a known criminal organization, you won't," Forbes said.

"Then why the hell would I admit to you I told them about the raid and implicate myself? Jesus, you two. Are you sure it's me fucking up your operation?"

"You're total garbage, Sorin. Curran's stuck her neck out for you and this is how you do her? All of us? We were a team and a few months ago there was nothing you wanted more than taking down the Rat Lords. What happened to you?" she said disgustedly.

I piled beans and sausage onto the bread and folded it up, cramming half of it into my mouth and mumbling around it, "I don't have anything to say to you, Monroe."

"Let's go, Mish." Forbes wrapped a huge arm around her shoulders. "We're wasting our time here."

"Yeah, Mish. Better go make some gains or something." I flexed my bicep.

I didn't see them again and suffered my last twenty-four hours in holding in silence. I had never seen the officer that opened the cell door to release me.

He grabbed my upper arm and guided me out of holding. "Your personal items are at the—"

"I know where they are."

I jerked my arm from his grip and walked down the hall to processing. I was the only one going in or out, but the dicks made me wait for twenty minutes anyway before dumping the contents of a large envelope with my name on it unceremoniously on the counter.

I signed for them and put on my watch and belt and jammed my wallet, keys, and boot laces into my pockets. My cash was gone. Assholes. There was a crumpled-up slip of paper with printed block letters.

If you want it back you're going to have to ask nicely

I sighed heavily and looked at the officer behind the counter expectantly.

"What?" he snapped.

"May I have my cue back?" I gritted my teeth. "Please."

He picked up the empty envelope and shook it over the table, before peering inside it. "Nope, not in here."

"Where the hell is it?"

"Why don't you check in evidence? Oh, right, you ain't a cop."

"It's in evidence?"

"How the hell should I know. Maybe you should go ask your Rat Lord buddies?"

I clucked my tongue. I got it. "You know, I may just do that. Thanks, dickhead."

Even after six hours of sleep, the longest hottest shower of my life, some eye makeup, and a double bacon cheeseburger, I was still feeling rocky after a blow to the head and three days in jail. The knot on my head had reduced considerably but had colored up nicely around my temple and left eye, making me look even more like the dropout I was.

I thought about strapping my subcompact Glock to my ankle, but going in there armed wasn't a good idea. I wasn't expecting trouble—yet. Instead, I jammed the three-inch auto knife with two-inch, spear-point blade Ray had given me for Christmas into my pocket. I really would be better off waiting until I was back in fighting form before walking into the lion's den—or the rat's nest. But, I mean, I had been invited. Right?

Any second thoughts I had I pushed aside while on the bus to the outskirts of the city. I was on my own now and stepped off into the dirt parking lot of the known Rat Lord's MC clubhouse—Boomer's Billiards. Without my police-issue unmarked I didn't have a car and I wasn't going to encourage anyone to track me down with an Uber account. I brushed some lint from the black suede jacket I added to my black jeans and cranberry short-sleeve button-down ensemble. Look good. Feel good.

The building was a long, one-story, metal-sided place with nothing memorable about it but the long line of Harleys parked neatly across the front with just enough space between them to walk through to the front door.

The inside was one giant cement-floored room the size of a basketball court with regulation-size, blue-cloth tables lined up evenly with enough room for high-top bar tables and stools between them. The walls were lined with racks of house cues, photos of bike rallies, celebrities, framed club jackets of lost members, and beer mirrors. The far wall was dotted with closed doors leading to who knew where—back door, office, storeroom, or washroom probably. The lighting was dim except over the tables, so those not right up at the table were hidden in shadow and there was hazy cast to the air from cigarette smoke. Apparently, Boomer hadn't gotten the memo about not smoking indoors.

To my right was a well-lit bar with built-in glass cabinets selling cues and Boomer's swag as well as beer and liquor. I assumed this was also where you rented a table. Behind the bar was a large, hairy, tattooed man of indeterminate age who looked like he'd excel at ZZ Top cosplay. His Boomer's T-shirt stretched across a thick chest and around arms as big around as my legs.

On the other side of the bar in the far corner was a private area separated from the main room by a half-wall. The center of the space was dominated by a gorgeous nine-foot Kim Steel competition table with matte black finish and blood-red cloth. The floor was tiled and the walls lined with lush gray leather furniture and low-end tables. The sofas were currently occupied by a handful of club members I recognized as top-ranking officers. If they had a record—and most of them did—I knew their face. I took it all in at a glance and didn't let my gaze linger.

I turned my attention back to the counter to see the big man leaning on his knuckles and staring when I approached. Be cool. Be cool.

"I know you?" he asked.

"Do you need to? I'm paying cash." I wasn't entirely sure how to play this and decided to come in snarky. Was there any other way? If that was a mistake I'd find out soon enough. I pulled a bill from my pocket and slid the folded hundred across the bar. Money talks, right?

He eyed it and snorted. "Who are you?"

"I'm well, thank you. I'd like a table for a few hours and a bucket of PBR, please and thank you."

His lip curled. "*Who* the hell are you?"

"Who the hell are *you*?" I held his glare without flinching. Maybe I *was* brain damaged from the blow to the head.

"The goddamn owner."

I failed to repress a snicker. "Okay, Boomer. A rack and a bucket of beer. Thanks."

Sadly, he didn't get the joke.

"Tables are full."

I already knew they weren't but turned and made a show of scanning the dim smoky room.

"Back off, Boomer. Don't you know who this is?" Shade walked over from the private table area. Her voice was exactly like you'd imagine—a dump truck driving over a gravel road.

Boomer sneered at me. "This little punk? Nah."

"This is Lucky Sorin. The ex-cop turned hustler Tommy's been going on about."

"From Chumps? Nah, it ain't. Tommy said she was a chick." He snorted at his own joke.

"Ha! Good one." I raised two fingers in a V to my mouth and wagged my tongue between them.

Boomer reddened and those near enough to hear erupted into coarse laughter at my mocking of him.

"Get the *chick* a beer, Boomer," the woman said and eyed me up and down. She clearly did not like what she saw.

"Whatever you say, Shade." He popped a PBR tall boy and cracked it on the bar, causing it to foam out the top.

I turned to grab my beer and a hand slammed into the middle of my back, throwing me forward. I banged into the bar with both hands, bracing myself as the woman leaned into me. She smelled of leather and smoke.

"I'm going to enjoy this," she hissed into my ear and kicked my legs apart.

"You wouldn't be the first." I tried to look as bored as possible while she patted me down, snaking her hands up under my shirt and down my pants, paying particular attention to my tits and crotch.

She kept a hand in the small of my back and pulled my knife from my pocket. She flicked it open right next to my ear to reveal the sharp but tiny two-inch blade. "What were you gonna do with this?"

"I take my contacts out with it."

She spun me around and pushed a hand into my chest, bending me backward over the counter and I couldn't help a grunt of surprise and pain. She was really strong. I froze when the point of my own knife pricked right under my chin and she pressed, forcing my head back uncomfortably. A trickle of blood crawled its way down my throat.

"You got a smart fuckin' mouth," she snarled. She held me like that for another long moment, a clear show of dominance. I didn't struggle, but I didn't look away either. She stepped back abruptly and slammed my knife down on the counter and called loudly to the room, "She's clean."

I straightened off the counter, fixed my rumpled clothes, and pocketed my knife. I finally picked up my beer and blew the foam off in Boomer's direction. I raised it to the scary woman staring at me and hid my nerves behind a long swallow. "Thanks, uh, Shade is it? That was my grandma's name, too."

She glowered. "Griff wants to talk to you."

"Who?"

"Yeah, right. Move your ass."

CHAPTER NINE

I had seen plenty of photos of Griffin Hillis, but they were all old mugshots of him bleary-eyed or beat up. As president he had others in the club doing the wet work now and personally hadn't seen the inside of a jail cell in years. Seeing him up close on his own turf was unexpected. He was clean shaven, with high cheekbones, broad features and a narrow mouth. His dark hair, streaked with gray, was thick and wavy and his deep-set eyes were intelligent and clear. By all accounts he should have been attractive, but I found him positively repulsive and worked very hard not to show it.

The clean-cut young guy looking like an Abercrombie model in a club leather vest was Freezone, the VP. The scrawny, weaselly looking guy with bad teeth next to him was Saint, the Sergeant at Arms. He should have been racking up five to ten for manslaughter when he drove a broken bottle through the throat of a local in a bar fight last year, but the case against him collapsed when the star witness died in the Cherry Hill apartment fire, which so far, we could not connect to the club at all. Making up the rest of the crowd were Beanie, Ghost, and

Mutant. All known to city cops, but they hadn't yet warranted more than a cursory look. So far.

Then there was the woman, Shade, who I had never seen mentioned in any of the task force's files. How she had stayed off anyone's radar was a mystery—or maybe just another case of the women being overlooked and underestimated. There was no reason that play shouldn't work just as well for the bad guys—or gals.

She was obviously high-ranking as she perched on the edge of the sofa and tangled her fingers in the long dark hair at the back of the neck of Mira Allen. I shouldn't have been surprised to see her, but I was. She stiffened at Shade's touch and I bristled on the inside but managed to keep my expression neutral. I hoped.

Mira was as gorgeous as ever with more understated makeup, in tight jeans and tight tank top, leaving little to the imagination. Her gaze cruised me slowly, but she gave away nothing with the look. Zero for two with the ladies today.

I turned my attention back to Griffin and made every effort to look relaxed when he pulled my cue from the case and screwed it together. He meant to intimidate and maybe I should have taken his cue—no pun intended—but I had no intention of submitting by pretending that I didn't notice. "That's mine."

He caressed the cue like a lover running a hand up a well-toned leg. "That's not asking nicely."

I straightened and cleared my throat. "Where *are* my manners? That's mine and I want it back."

"It's beautiful." He grinned and chalked the tip. "I think I'll keep it."

"No. You won't."

The only one who didn't laugh at that was Mira. Griffin cocked his head at the challenge. "So, arrest me for stealing."

I stiffened when he leaned my cue against the wall—no one leans my cue against the wall—and began to rack the balls.

"Oh, right, you can't. You got drummed out of your own unit for, what was that I heard, conduct unbecoming? They do that to your face, too?"

I touched the still tender bruise at the side of my head. "This happened after I told your boy Tommy about the raid about to go down at Chumps. How did he get out anyway? I can't imagine the cops didn't have the exits covered."

"I can't give away *all* my secrets." He lifted the diamond off a tight nine-ball rack.

"How did you even get my cue? It was on the bar when the cops showed up."

He shrugged. "Like I already said. But I'll tell you what, because you got sack comin' in here and because you did me a solid, how about we play for it. One game, winner takes all. You win and you get to walk out of here with your cue."

"And if I lose?"

"You *crawl* out of here—if you're able—and I keep your stick. Or, you can turn around right now and walk away without it, unharmed. Sound fair?"

My gaze flicked to Mira Allen who offered me a small shake of her head. I wasn't sure how to interpret that, but I chose to imagine she wanted me to walk away to avoid getting hurt. And I had no doubt Griffin *would* hurt me if he wanted to, regardless of who won the game. The question was, how committed was I to my course of action and how much did I care one way or the other?

"You got a cue for me to use?" I kept my expression carefully neutral when his brows went up. He had expected me to walk away and I cheered inwardly. I was already in his head.

"Ghost, give her the L28."

The tall guy with the neck tats and three-day stubble pulled a McDermott maple cue with Irish linen wrap off the rack. It wasn't mine, but it was a good starter cue and I had run tables with far worse. In college I won a bar game with a broom handle like that scene with Kevin Costner in *Tin Cup*.

"Thank you." I was happy with the weight, the tip was good and the shaft straight. I took my jacket off and hung it on the back of a chair and looked at Griffin expectantly.

"Guests break." He gestured grandly to the table.

I tuned out everything else and chalked the cue, breathing deeply in through my nose and out through my mouth to slow my heart, as I rolled the cue ball into position. I bridged the cue across the rail and slid the shaft between my fingers, feeling the wood warm against my skin with each stroke. I hit the cue ball hard and fast and it cracked into the one-ball and exploded the rack, sending the nine-ball firing into the corner pocket ending the game. I won. I exhaled and stood slowly, waiting for the total silence to die down.

Griffin barked a laugh. "Did I say one game? I meant two out of three. You rack."

"Sure." I pulled the balls I dropped from the pockets and dropped them into the rack—the one-ball in front and the nine in the middle—tightening them with my fingers at the edges before lifting the rack off. As the winner of the previous game he should have been racking and me breaking, but now was not the time to quibble over the rules.

I cringed inwardly when he lined up to break with my custom cue. If he was planning on beating me up, the least he could do was break with a house cue and preserve my tip. His break was strong and he sank the two and seven ball, scattering the rest and leaving the nine-ball hanging so close to the corner pocket a stiff breeze might knock it in.

The one, three and four-ball sat open at the opposite end and he dropped them without hesitation, but left himself out of position for the five. He attempted an impossible shot, and predictably, missed.

I chalked my cue and ran the table, leaving only the eight sitting tight against the rail and the nine hanging in the corner pocket. The cue ball sat at the opposite end of the table.

"There's a lot of cloth between you and that win," Griffin said.

"Yeah." I chalked up again and pointed the cue down the table. "Off the eight, nine in the corner." I didn't need to call my shot, but I wasn't sure what rules I was playing by—if any. This would all be over in ten more seconds one way or another.

"Kitten," he said. "Help me out and give Lucky here something else to think about. Do that fucking thing we saw in that dumb old Robin Hood movie."

Mira Allen rose to her feet like a predatory cat and glided toward the table like I was lunch. I'd allow it. She towered over me in four-inch wedge sandals and I couldn't help but take her in slowly from head to toe, trying not to linger too long on any one feature despite all of them deserving more time. To be fair, though, no one wore a black and chrome, mudflap girl belt buckle that shiny and that low on their hips, if they didn't want folks looking. It was like she won top prize in roping at an erotic rodeo, and I was here for it. She brushed her hair from her shoulders and I caught the subtle scent of florals and musk.

She spoke for my ears alone. "Take your shot. I won't touch you."

"I'm sorry to hear that." My quip was rewarded with a small quirk of her mouth.

I lined up and Mira bent over at the waist, her full breasts a hairsbreadth from my bridge arm and her mouth an inch from my ear. My head swam with her nearness, the warmth from her body and her scent filling me with every inhale.

As I pulled back the cue to take the shot, I shivered at Mira's warm breath against my ear. I raised my head and turned toward her and my lips grazed hers, sending a jolt of electricity down my body. I exhaled, our breath mingling, and shot without looking. The cue ball rolled with the sweetest touch and just kissed the eight ball before tapping the nine into the pocket, then stopping less than an inch from a scratch.

I held Mira's hooded gaze and straightened, licking my lips for one last taste of her. She was still so close I could feel the heat of her and see her pulse jumping in her neck. I stepped away and placed the borrowed cue on the table. The air was thick with danger and I waited while Griffin Hillis's face registered first surprise, then anger, and finally settled on amusement. He threw his head back and roared with laughter, giving permission for the rest of the group to laugh as well.

I shrugged and smiled as I whipped my jacket back on. "Thanks for the game. I'll let you get back to it." I gestured for my cue.

He eyed it, then with two hands handed it over with a deep bow. "I am nothing if not a man of my word and you, Lucky Sorin, are an intriguing woman. Stay and play another game."

I unscrewed my cue and slipped it back into the case. "Thank you, no. I have some things I need to take care of."

"That wasn't a suggestion."

I stilled and met his gaze. I would not bow to this man. "Another time, then."

His smile didn't reach his eyes. "I'll hold you to that."

I'm gonna call that a win. It was time to go and I headed for the door. I knew he wasn't going to let me beat him and then leave unscathed. I expected to be struck from behind any second and was so tense I jumped when he spoke again.

"Oh, by the way, Lucky. Can I call you Lucky? You haven't seen Sky Kingston around, have you? I know you two are friends. Got any idea where she is? It's been a minute and I miss that little piece."

I went rigid, the heat of rage flaming up to color my neck and face. I would have rather he hit me. I had expected his parting shot to be physical and I was wrong. He was in my head, too. "She's dead."

"Oh. I'm sorry to hear that. How?"

"OD." I tore my eyes from Hillis and looked to Mira whose face had gone ashen, her eyes bright with emotion. There was a loose thread there. If I picked at it perhaps it would unravel and give me something I could work with. I banged out the door and took what felt like my first full breath since I walked in.

CHAPTER TEN

Hey, Google, what's the appropriate amount of time to wait before walking back into a criminal biker gang's clubhouse at the president's vague and sinister invitation? Three days? Great. That's what I was thinking.

This time, in addition to the little knife in my pocket, I strapped my little Glock to my right calf just above my boot, making sure I could pull my pant leg up in a hurry. Here's to hoping I only ever needed a little bit of help.

The pool hall was hopping today with all but a few of the tables in use and the private area dark and empty. Huh. Wonder if those things are connected—when the cat's away and all. It came as no surprise as there were only a handful of bikes parked in front. The regular clientele looked unremarkable for a pool hall. Mostly men of the jeans and T-shirt variety and a few women scattered around and there were no club patches showing. The cracking of pool balls was the loudest sound.

"You again." Boomer's copious facial hair rippled in my direction.

"Boomer." I gave him a nod. "Bucket of PBR and a table. Please and thank you."

He made me wait a long time before pulling a battered tin pail from beneath the counter and dragging it through the ice bin. He dropped it onto the counter and jammed five cans into it.

"Thank you." When it didn't look like he was going to move again without some encouragement, I pulled two twenties from my pocket and slid them across the counter. His eyes flicked to them and then returned to stare me down. "Really, man? Is it me?"

"Yes."

I dug out two more twenties and handed them over and he produced a rack of balls and two nubs of chalk. "Thanks. You're a peach."

I chose a table against the wall so I could see the entire room, including the VIP area. I hadn't even racked the balls when the club returned. The rumble was loud and long as nearly all of them rolled in from their ride. I feigned disinterest while they filed into the building. Leather creaked, buckles jangled and the smell of leather, sweat, and exhaust overpowered even cigarette smoke for a minute.

The club members were hard to tell apart, all in denim and leather, tattooed and hairy. They scattered to belly up to the bar or fill up empty tables. No one noticed me and it was easy to stand back against the wall in the shadows and watch them.

Tommy Pringle came in with a group, laughing and gesturing wildly. They headed to the bar where Boomer was handing out booze. Tommy turned from the counter and looked right at me. Busted. I went back to the table and finished racking the balls.

He came over and hoisted one leg onto a chair nearby. "You got a death wish, kid?"

"I was invited." I pulled a house cue off the wall to break.

"Yeah, but you weren't actually supposed to come."

The cue cracked into the balls, which barely scattered far enough to hit a rail. I scowled. "Loose rack."

"I heard about your match with Griffin the other day. Bold move."

"What, winning?"

"Coming in here."

I shrugged. "I needed my cue."

The rumble of bike engines grew loud again and then cut off. The officers came in, Freezone, Ghost, Beanie, Saint, and Shade. Last in was Griffin with his arm around the neck of Mira Allen—tight jeans, tighter T-shirt and leather jacket. She was windblown and sexy as hell. She didn't wear a club patch. Interesting. She started to pull away from him but Griffin's arm tightened around her neck and pulled her close for a bruising kiss.

I tensed, my grip tightening around the cue when her hands flew up to press against his chest, but stopped just short of pushing him away. He was hurting her. He let her go with a smack on her ass and a push toward the back of the room. The others laughed and moved toward the bar, except for Freezone and Ghost, who walked to the back with her, each with a hand on her back the whole way.

She must have felt the weight of my stare and turned to look. A flicker of surprise and then anger crossed her face before she looked away. She pushed open an unmarked door at the back of the room and disappeared with the two men following right behind.

Tommy snorted. "You ain't *that* lucky. Don't even think about it."

Tommy's warning startled me. I'd forgotten he was there. "No worries. I never think about anything."

"No shit."

The rest of the officers headed to the back of the room with their drinks and went through a door marked *Private*. "Board meeting?" I asked.

His eyes narrowed. "Thought you weren't on the job no more."

"Just curious." I went back to my game and tried not to think about what was going on behind closed doors.

The time did not pass idly by. Every stinking Rat Lords member in the place wanted to take a crack at beating me. I was like the sword in the fucking stone. They were even placing bets like it was a goddamn cock fight—which, it was. *And* they drank my beer. Better than beating the piss out of me, though I'd like to think I could take more than a few of them in a brawl. I mean, not at the same time.

My next shot put me facing the doors at the back in time to see Freezone and Ghost come out adjusting themselves while Mira was holding the door wearing nothing but a T-shirt that barely covered her. My anger flared and I hit the cue ball so hard it jumped the table, giving the men a laugh.

I pushed her out of my mind and gave them another hour of my undivided attention. Some of them weren't half bad and a couple of times I caught myself having a good time before I remembered my place. I didn't think they were going to let me go until I lost, so I did.

I put on a good show before getting distracted and miscuing on what should have been an easy bank. "Motherfucker!"

The room erupted into cheers and everyone started chanting, "Slug. Slug. Slug." Presumably my thick-necked, slightly hunched, opponent's name.

I timed my carefully crafted *error* while playing someone I deemed worthy of the win. Slug did me proud by running out, and defeated, I headed to the bar propelled by a few sympathetic back slaps.

"Finally got put in your place, huh?" Boomer smirked.

"Mm, yeah, your boy Slug sure showed me. How about a drink to soothe my wounded pride?"

He popped a PBR and poured me a shot of tequila. "Pity shot. On me."

I nodded my thanks and drank it down, regretting it immediately. Fucking bottom shelf bullshit Montezuma White. I coughed and guzzled my beer. "Thanks, asshole."

He barked a laugh, enjoying watching me suffer while the shot slowly sanitized my digestive tract.

"Hey, Boomer, how are you?"

I didn't see her until she leaned on the bar next to me, soothing my corroded nasal passages with her scent. It was the first I'd heard her normal speaking voice and it was exactly as I'd imagined—silvery smoke.

Apparently, I wasn't the only one susceptible to her sorcery. Boomer went from prickly to posh in an instant. He straightened up, hoisted his pants, and raked crumbs from his beard. Jesus.

"How's that monster treating you today?" he asked, his eyes twinkling.

I made no effort to hide my shock at their interaction and my gaze flicked between them.

Mira slid keys across the counter and flashed him a charming smile. "Purring like a kitten. Thank you for sharing your precious with me."

He grinned back like a teenage boy after his first real kiss and covered her hand and the keys with a meaty paw. "Oh, why don't you hang onto those for me."

"Are you sure?"

He blushed. "You know I can't ride no more 'cause of my sciatica. That Road King ain't gonna ride itself. Guess maybe now I should call it a Road Queen."

He giggled at his own joke and my jaw dropped.

"Thanks, Boo, you're the best." She leaned across the bar and planted a quick kiss on his cheek before pocketing the keys.

"My pleasure." He finally caught on to my barely contained amusement at the scene and cleared his throat, his expression turning hard again. "What can I get ya, doll?"

"You have any of the Warbler Pale left?"

"Sure do. I keep a secret stash just for you. Be right back." He lumbered off.

I clucked my tongue. "That was adorable. He lets you ride his bike?"

She arched a brow. "For a handy once a week."

I choked on my beer. "No."

Her laughter was magical. "Of course, not. He's my father."

"What?" I gaped at her. "He is not."

"You're cute."

"You're lying."

"Not about you being cute."

"About what then?"

Before she could answer Boomer returned with her beer, setting the bottle down carefully. "Here you go, Mira."

"Thank you, Boomer." She waited for him to move off. "He's not my father. And the only thing of his I'll ever be straddling is that bike and he knows it. Caught him sniffing the seat once after I borrowed it for a ride, though. That's as close to this"—she swept a graceful hand up and down her body—"as he's ever gonna get."

I groaned. "Please, stop. I can't hear anymore."

She grinned and raised her bottle to me. "You asked."

"Guess those other two guys earlier were allowed to get up close and personal? Don't you want something stronger to wash the taste out of your mouth?" I asked like a dickhead. I was trying to rattle her.

She arched a brow at me, unfazed, and sipped her beer. "Sometimes I wrap it in a fruit roll-up if it's a ripe one."

Oh god. Was there nothing I could say to knock her off her game? "That's so nasty."

She smirked, knowing she got to me again. "Jealous? I don't discriminate. In fact, I prefer women—so much softer and sweeter."

The private door at the back opened and Shade stalked out, malice pouring off her with every stride. Jesus. She really should have her own villain music, like Darth Vader or Michael Meyers. Mira visibly shuddered and turned away from her. "Except for her. That one's poison through and through," she said quietly.

Shade made her feelings clear as she headed to the front door. The look she shot me suggested she'd like to knit my entrails into a scarf. When she turned her attention to Mira the hate in her eyes turned to a lust so powerful I nearly felt violated by it.

"Jesus Christ. She's scary," I muttered.

"You have no idea." Mira turned toward me and looked me over. "So, how about it?"

"What?"

"Would you care for a romp?"

Would I? My insides turned inside out and my mouth went dry, but she wasn't part of the plan. "I'll let you in on a secret about me. I don't pay for sex."

She shrugged. "Suit yourself, Lucky. What's your real name, anyway?"

"Lucky is my real name?"

"I mean the name on your driver's license."

"Why is the name given to me by people who don't even know me more real than the one I chose for myself?"

"Your parents are people who don't know you?"

"As a matter of fact, yes."

"Really? That's kinda sad."

"And you're kinda judgy for a hooker."

"Sex worker." She waved at Boomer. "Can I get another beer?"

"Why do you do it?" I asked.

"I'm good at it. We all have our gifts and mine make me a hundred bucks an hour."

"And Griffin Hillis is what, your pimp?"

"Not that it's any of your business, but Griff saved me, literally saved me when he stopped a guy from beating the shit out of me. I came out of a really messed up long-term relationship. I'd only been on my own a couple months and was making some poor choices. Anyway, he took care of me. Gave me a place, some clothes, helped me find work."

"If hanging with this crowd is a step up for you, I don't even wanna know what choices you consider *poor*. But, just to be clear, you know, a blow job isn't actually a job, right?"

"Now who's judgy? And I'm pretty sure I shouldn't be taking career counseling from the woman hustling a living by poking balls around."

"Guess we have that in common." I tapped my beer can against her bottle. "How long ago was that?"

"What?"

"That Griffin took you in?"

"One year, two weeks, and three days, but who's counting?"

"Don't you want something else? Something more?"

She laughed humorlessly but couldn't meet my eyes. "What more could I possibly want?"

My nerves were jangling and every alarm bell was going off. I was treading on dangerous ground, but I couldn't stop myself. I gripped her hand. "I can help you, Mira."

She met my gaze and I could see the longing in them, not for me, but for something more. Something safe. Her gaze darted over my shoulder and her eyes flashed with fear before she jerked her hand out of mine.

I never saw the slap coming and it snapped my head around so hard I thought my neck might break. The crack it made was loud enough to turn heads and there was total silence followed by a ripple of laughter.

"Watch your damn mouth. Don't you know where you are?" Mira spat and shook out her hand.

I rubbed my hot, stinging cheek. That was gonna leave a mark. "What the hell was that for?"

She lowered her voice. "There are cameras everywhere. I don't know what game you're playing, but you're going to get us both killed. Don't try to get close to me. Don't even come back here."

Guess I'd overstayed my welcome today. Or overplayed my hand. Probably both.

CHAPTER ELEVEN

Hey, Google, how long before you go back into the heart of the criminal organization responsible for the death of your friend to see a woman who bitch-slapped you to put some distance between you for both your safety and hers? Twenty-four hours? That's what I thought.

With a little handgun, little knife, and little confidence in what I was doing, I took a cab today and paid cash, of course. At my request he passed Boomer's slowly, ensuring the bikes were out front. I had no idea how many were there on the regular, but it looked like a lot were there now. There was no club ride going on. He dropped me several hundred yards up the road at my request.

I was barely two minutes into my walk when I heard the rumble of engines from behind me. I couldn't tell who the riders were from a distance or if they were even part of the club and they didn't acknowledge me at all. They blew by me and disappeared around a slow bend to the left and were soon out of sight and hearing.

From my satellite images search I knew the way the road curved and this walk would take me to the back of the building. An easy and innocent enough way to get my eyes on the rest of the landscape. From as far away as I could stand and still see, I scanned the back and saw one dome camera over a single steel door on the right side of the building. Probably motion activated with a range of at least twenty yards. The door would be the entrance to the boardroom, or whatever they called it. There was a well-maintained, paved parking area off the door with a drive that went around the building on that side. Clearly, it was used for something. Fortunately, no one was using it now.

The rest of the rear of the building was as expected with an overflowing dumpster and a crumbling concrete pad with a basketball hoop missing the net. The ground surrounding it was gravel and dirt littered with bike parts, beer cans, and cigarette butts—classic.

I stayed well out of range of the dome camera and made my way closer to the back of the building. In the middle of the back wall was the air-conditioning unit and the water meter. Six feet from the ground were two awning windows corresponding, as far as I could tell, with the space Mira was using, for whatever it was she did. That window was open and I could just make out music. Halsey, maybe.

On the far left just before the corner opposite the meeting room, were two more small windows I knew were for the men's and women's restroom, or rather, the men's and men's overflow. Very few women were ever at Boomer's and I suspected the ones that were avoided needing the restroom at all costs. I, for one, would rather piss in the parking lot than ever go in there again.

Which is why, when women's voices drifted out the window as I made my way around the side, I had to stop. Mira and Shade. Damn it, now I was going to have to eavesdrop outside a restroom like some pervy stalker. I stepped up right against the building beneath the open window.

"What are we doing in here, Mira? Thought you were disgusted by this place."

"I am. Seems appropriate, though, and I wanted this to be private."

Shade's gravelly laugh made me flinch. "If you wanted some private time you could have just invited me to your room."

"No, thanks."

"Oh, I see. That look of disgust isn't for the toilets. It's for the company."

"You said it, not me."

Atta girl, Mira. I cheered inwardly and wished I could be a fly on that bathroom wall right now. I guess this was the next best thing save for being able to see the expression on Shade's face while she got shut down.

"Sure, Mira, you've got standards, I guess. But you've got no problem getting spit-roasted by Ghost and Freezone every other day."

Oh, gross, and just, no. Please, don't let that image stay with me long.

"Think what you want, Shade, but you and I are never going to happen."

"Then stop wasting my time. What do you want?"

"You know what I want. Take it off."

"Now you're talking, sweet cheeks."

"The necklace, Shade. Take it off."

"What's it to you?"

I've never wanted to smack the smug smirk, that I could only imagine her making, off someone's face so bad in my life.

"I'll go to Griffin. He'll make you—"

"Are you really that naive, Mira? Go ahead and run crying to him. He'll do shit. You've been around long enough to know Griffin Hillis is a figurehead. A show pony. He doesn't run this club. I do. And everyone knows it. You think it was Griffin who cleaned up that manslaughter charge for Saint?"

Oh, shit. The Street Crimes Unit wasn't even looking at Shade for the Cherry Hill Apartments fire. If we even knew her name before now it hadn't been shared. Up until now she'd just been background noise. I needed to get back to the gym and use the phone. If the unit started picking at that thread maybe something would unravel. It was quiet for so long I wondered if Mira had left.

"You started that fire? People died, Shade. Children died."

"Like I already asked. What's it to you?"

"Nothing. Forget it. I'm out."

There was movement, shuffling feet and an opening door.

"Where do you think you're going? I'm not done." The door slammed closed again.

"Well, I am. Get your hands off me, Shade."

"Settle down, Mira. You want something from me? I want something from you. Simple."

"No!"

Ah, damn. That's my cue. No pun intended. I pushed off the wall and jogged around the building to the front.

Slug and Tommy were leaning against their bikes talking with a guy I hadn't seen before. Big and bald with a tattoo on the back of his head. Oh, shit, it's him.

"Hey, Lucky!" Tommy called. "Come meet Thor. Been telling him about you. He wants a game."

Thor, of course that's his name. I paused at the door and sketched a wave. Guy had a long goatee in multiple braids and arms as big around as my head. No time for him right now. "Gotta hit the loo. Sorry."

It was a full house for club members. The tables nearest the bar were all in use and the private area was full with the officers. There weren't many, or any, patrons beyond that. Freezone saw me first and gave Griffin a nudge. Griffin's mouth quirked in greeting and he beckoned me over.

I offered him my most apologetic smile and did a little shuffling dance between the tables as I made my way to the back of the building where a narrow hallway led to the restrooms. I'm sure it hadn't taken much more than a minute for me to get there from around back, but it seemed like much longer. I took a deep breath and banged through the door just in time to see Mira shove Shade hard enough to send her staggering backward into a stall door with a bang and string of swears. Atta girl.

"Whoa." I looked between them as Shade straightened, red-faced and furious. She had three bleeding scratches across her chest. "Sorry. Am I interrupting?"

"This isn't over, Mira."

Mira's eyes flashed angrily. "It is for me."

Shade's hate-filled gaze flicked from Mira to me. "What the fuck are you doing here?"

I shrugged innocently. "I gotta go."

Her lip curled menacingly and she very blatantly sized me up then arched a brow in Mira's direction.

"Shade, don't." Mira looked from Shade to me, her eyes wide and fearful.

"Don't what?" I really wasn't playing dumb now. I was not catching on to whatever had just been communicated.

"Mira here got me all revved up but now she doesn't want to play. So maybe I have some fun with you and burn off some excess energy."

Uh-oh. "Um, no thank you."

"You gotta piss?" She advanced on me. "How 'bout I give you a hand and beat it outta you?"

"Wait. What?" I backed up and fumbled for the door. "That doesn't sound like very much fun for me."

"Shade, no!" Mira yelled as I made it back through the bathroom door loudly and with a great deal of panic.

"You had your chance, Mira." Shade said as she followed me out. "This bitch wants to hang with us, then she plays by our rules." She raised her voice as I backed my way down the narrow hall. "And we all know the rules, don't we, boys?"

All eyes were on us when we emerged into open space, with many of the club moving in closer, curiosity turning to anticipation on their faces. Voices were raised and money started changing hands. This was bad.

"What rules? I don't know the rules." I lifted my cue case from across my shoulders and set it on an empty table. I had a pretty good idea what was about to happen.

"Someone fill *un*-Lucky here on Mira's number one rule," Shade called out.

Slug bounced up and down on his toes, excitedly while he shouted, "No one interrupts when a club member is with Mira."

Shade grinned and continued to close the distance between us. The first step in self-defense is situational awareness. I was all too aware the situation was about to go to hell real fast. I was not among friends, and there was nowhere left for me to go as the men closed us in on all sides. Shit. Shit. Shit.

Mira gripped Shade's arm to hold her back. "We were just talking. We weren't doing anyth—"

"I say we were. And *she* interrupted." Shade shoved Mira away and glanced past me. I turned to follow her gaze, catching the nod from Griffin.

Pain ripped across my face from her solid right cross before I'd even turned all the way back to face her. Cheating bitch. I staggered but didn't go down. Blood filled my mouth and I spat on the floor. "Fuck you," I growled.

The men howled with laughter.

"Watch out, Shade. She's a cop," someone snickered.

"Don't mean she can fight," someone called back.

They weren't wrong. The academy taught restraint holds and the bare minimum of self-defense. Basically, just enough to make rookies think they knew something about fighting and land them in the hospital after their first scuffle. I'd seen it before.

Guess that was why Angela thought I'd be right for this gig. I'd been street brawling my whole life. Keep moving, hurt them before they hurt you, and get away. I had the philosophy down long before I knew there was someone who could teach me to fight and that it had a name. Krav Maga.

I widened my stance and bent my knees, left leg forward and right back, both feet pointing toward Shade and my hands up, palms open. It may look odd, but a strike with the heel of my hand could do serious damage and lessened my chance of getting hurt when I connected with her stupid sneering face.

Someone behind me made an obnoxious kung-fu sound effect that had the men laughing.

"Sweep the leg, Shade!" someone hollered.

Shade snorted a laugh and wasted time showing off for the club, raising her arms to get them cheering. She'd already gotten in one cheap shot and I wasn't going to let her get in another.

I rushed her fast with a left-hand strike to the throat followed by a hard-right elbow to her face that snapped her head back with a strangled gasp. I grabbed her wrist and pulled her into a basic side clinch. My left hand hooked under her right arm and right arm curled around the back of her neck, bending her toward me to break her posture and control her body. I drove my right knee hard into her midsection once, twice, three times until I felt her knees buckle. She dropped at my feet with a wheeze, her legs kicking weakly as she struggled for breath.

I exhaled loudly, my heart pounding. My trainer would be proud. Except now I may have just screwed myself out of any chance to assist in the case, or to keep breathing. I was already on pretty shaky ground with this crowd. How favorably were they going to look on me after I destroyed one of their officers in a matter of seconds?

I searched the awed faces to find Mira's, hoping for some answers. She stared at me, coolly, her expression revealing nothing until her eyes widened in alarm and her lips parted to speak.

Pain in my head exploded and I dropped where I stood, my arms and legs numb to my commands. A trickling warmth ran through my hair and dripped down the back of my neck. My collar was getting damp. Shade stood over me, holding her middle and sucking in deep ragged breaths. She dropped the eight ball she'd apparently crashed into my skull next to my head. It cracked against the floor and rolled away. "I'll kill you for this," she snarled.

I groaned, my vision drifting in and out of focus and my hold on reality questionable. I had no clever retorts. No defense. No last words. Their words floated around me like a dream sequence.

"Back off, Shade, and let me think."

"Fuck, Griff, we ain't really gonna kill her, are we?"

"She's a cop."

"She ain't a cop."

"Thor'll take care of it. He always does."

I couldn't make out who was talking and just tried to concentrate on getting back control of my body without crying or throwing up.

"You two shit-for-brains don't get a vote." Shade's voice was unmistakable. "Griff, you've had your fun with this bitch. Let's bury her and be done with it."

"Griff, please." Mira's voice cut through the haze of confusion and pain. "You don't want this kind of trouble. You have to let her—" Her voice cut out with a shriek.

I rolled my eyes toward her. Hillis had threaded his hand through her hair and jerked her head back. "You don't ever tell me what to do," he hissed in her face.

Mira's face twisted in pain, but she didn't struggle against his grip. Bile rose in my throat when her hands slid over his crotch, kneading between his legs.

"Please, baby, we don't want a dead cop on our hands—ex or not." She nibbled around behind his ear. "They'll come looking and we don't want that kind of attention."

Hillis sighed contentedly at her ministrations. "On that we agree. Thor, get her out of here."

"Not so lucky anymore, huh?" Thor wasted no time grabbing me by the boot and dragging me toward the door. I didn't have the strength to stop him.

"Wait!" Mira said and laughed. "What are you going to do? Drag her out to the parking lot in the middle of the afternoon? She's barely conscious. You know patrols drive up and down this road a dozen times a day. Wouldn't they just love to see this. She has to be able to at least walk out of here on her own."

"She's got a point, Griff," Freezone said. "Her blood's all over the place. Never shit where you eat."

Hillis tightened his grip on Mira and closed his mouth over her gasp of pain, kissing her roughly and for a long time. When he finally released her, she staggered away slightly, her eyes wide and mouth bruised.

"Never can say no to you, kitten," he laughed. "Do with her as you wish. As soon as she can walk, show her the door. We know where she lives and who her friends are. We'll discuss what's to be done with her after that. She may still be of some use to us."

"We don't need her," Boomer said. "We've still got an inside—"

"Shut your hole, Boomer, before I shut it for you," Hillis barked. "Officer's meeting. Now."

My eyes drifted closed with relief. I wouldn't exactly say my cover was blown as much as my time undercover may have come to an unceremonious end, but I would live to see another day. Unfortunately, I would never see who was behind the boot to my face.

CHAPTER TWELVE

I'm near certain I never lost complete consciousness, but for the life of me I couldn't remember how I got from the floor outside the restrooms to the bed I was propped up in now. My head was cold and wet. My tongue felt thick. Water was running, soft music was playing from somewhere nearby and beneath that I could hear the rumble and murmur of voices—sometimes raised. I strained my senses, but my head pounded, making my ears ring and my vision cloudy.

I groaned with the effort of pushing myself farther up against the pillows behind me. My head felt double its natural size and my stomach flipped over at the motion. The water shut off and I turned slowly in the direction I heard the sound. From the other side of a flowing curtain to my left stepped Mira Allen and my heart gave a little lurch. I didn't yet know if it was a good or bad thing to be alone with her. But if I was going to be stuck at Boomer's for a while longer this was the safest place for me. For the moment, at least.

The concern and relief etched on her face at seeing me sitting up gave way to obvious frustration and anger and I rethought that sentiment. Just because my body wanted her body did not make her one of the good guys. She held a bowl of water and the small bed bent in when she sat down next to me, rocking me even closer to her. Our thighs touching made me forget all about the pain in my head, but gave me a new ache.

"I told you not to come back here." She set down the bowl and wrung out a cloth. "Hold still."

Being this near to her, under the weight of her hand against the side of my neck and her careful scrutiny of my face, I could do nothing but exactly what she said while she ran the cool cloth over me. I winced as she dabbed at my lips, wiping away enough blood to tinge the water pink when she rinsed it. I ran my tongue around the inside of my mouth and could feel the sting of small lacerations and taste the blood. No loose teeth, though, and nothing that needed stitches as far as I could tell.

"Yeah, well…" I mumbled in a poor excuse for an answer, unsure what the rest of that sentence sounded like. My brains seemed well and truly scrambled. Whether from the blows to the head or being this near Mira had yet to be determined. Focus, woman.

She dropped the cloth back into the bowl and pinned me with an impatient stare. "Yeah, well, what?"

I didn't have a line prepared and I couldn't hold her gaze. Some fucking undercover officer I was. I looked around the small space to buy some time. I was still with it enough to know I was in deep shit and my only way out of this room was either past—or through—Mira Allen.

I was laying atop a single bed, comfortable and nicely made. Above me on the wall were two bookshelves lined with books whose titles I couldn't read from where I was, and probably couldn't read if it was right in front of me. My vision was still whacked. Concussed, no doubt. With the curtain pulled aside now I could just see a small sink, toilet and narrow shower stall. On the other side of a second curtain was a small sitting room with a futon and coffee table. Was that where she, ahem, entertained?

She got up and dropped the bowl and cloth into the sink. She held up a bottle of ibuprofen. At least so far, she seemed to be on my side. I was going to have to take the chance and just go for it.

"Please. Thank you." I popped them into my mouth with a shaky hand and chased them with the half-finished bottle of water she handed me. "You live here?"

"It's not forever."

"For how long?" My head was clearing.

"Why the interest?" She crossed her arms and leaned a hip against the sink.

"I can help you. Help you get out of here." I swung my legs around and sat at the edge of the bed, carefully hiding my discomfort. I probed the back of my head, feeling the tender knot surrounding a small laceration that had fortunately stopped bleeding. I needed her to trust me and believe I could protect her even though she just watched me get my head nearly caved in by that cheap-shotting bitch.

Krav Maga was an amazing defense system, but the whole point was to strike first, fast and hard, and then run like hell. I got the *first* and *hard* part down, but had nowhere to go. What was I gonna do? Take them all on? Never should have turned my back on Shade, though. That one was on me.

She didn't even try to hide her dislike of my weak-ass offer of help. "You're starting to sound like a cop."

"*Ex*-cop," I insisted and looked anywhere but at her face, fixating on the small nightstand with a bottle of lube, half-burned candle, a couple of condoms, and a set of handcuffs and keys. Kinky.

"So you keep saying. You know you're on the fast track to be ex-breathing."

Probably, but if there was still a chance I could pull this off, I was going to try. "If Griffin wanted me dead he would have killed me already. Why hasn't he?"

"He keeps people around that are useful to him in some way. Get him what he wants. Money, power, information, drugs."

"Sex?"

She shrugged. "That, too."

"What's he get from me then?"

She shook her head and looked away for a long moment before turning back to me. She really was stunning and she smelled amazing. "Amusement. And when he gets bored of you, you'll find out personally where the bodies are buried. But it will be too late for you to tell anyone."

"That what they're discussing next door? How to dispose of my body?"

She barked a laugh. "Likely. Yet you seem unfazed."

"You didn't answer my question."

"What question?"

"You're a smart woman. Resourceful. Capable. Why do you stay here?"

Her eyes blazed fire and she took a step toward me. "Stop making the mistake of thinking I need saving. It's pissing me off."

"Still not an answer."

"I don't owe you any answers. But it won't be much longer until I can get clear from this rat hole."

"What are you waiting for?"

"The right time." Her gaze darted to the bookshelf above my head and then back to me so fast I almost missed it.

"Which is?"

"When I decide and not before. So, don't go thinking you're doing me any favors by causing trouble for me to get me to go."

I gave her my most innocent smile. "Why would you think I would do something like that?"

Her eyes narrowed. "Because I know your type."

"Oh, yeah?"

"Brought up rough. Fighting tooth and nail for everything you've got—which probably isn't much. Now you got all sharp edges, sharp wit, sharp tongue, and a big ol' soft heart for folks you think didn't get whatever chance someone gave you to turn it around."

Huh. She had me there. "You're smart."

"That's not me, Lucky. I'm not your new charity case, so don't waste your time here. Sky's dead. Nothing you're thinking about doing is going to change that."

I stiffened at the mention of her and my head throbbed in time with my pulse. "You knew her."

Her expression softened, her eyes shining with emotion. "I knew her. Good kid. This place was killing her and I tried to help her get out. Gave her money and tried to hook her up with the right people. Let her crash in the other room when she needed to. But she just kept coming back. She told me there was someone on the outside that was counting on her. Someone that was going to help her if she could just…"

Grief and shame at my failure crawled through my chest and squeezed my heart. "Oh, god. That was me."

"No shit. You think anyone here doesn't already know that?" Mira's expression turned fierce. "And look how that turned out for Sky. And the result isn't looking great for you either. So, you know I'm not bullshitting you when I say, stay off my side."

I blinked stupidly at her. Of course, they knew about my connection to Sky. "Why would Griffin even let me in here if he knows who I am? Hell, he invited me."

She laughed humorlessly and shook her head. "To torment you. He's a sociopath. That's what he does."

I shuddered inwardly. "I thought I amused him."

Her expression was chilling. "You think you're here for your scintillating wit? Your *pain* is what he enjoys."

I wanted to believe I still had some semblance of control over this situation. "You know Griffin had Sky killed. Or Shade did."

"Who do you think you're talking to? I know *everything*." She raked her hands through her hair. "And when he's done fucking with your head they'll kill you, too. But not before they hurt you."

I believed her and I needed her. "Then help me bring him down. All of them." I pushed myself to my feet and planted them wide to keep from toppling over. My head felt wobbly and my body weak. Shit.

She crossed her arms, her expression smug. "*Ex*-cop, huh?"

"I still…know people…and there's a phone…" Was I slurring?

"Jesus, Lucky."

Her arms went around me a second before I lost control of my legs and crumpled to the floor. She eased me back onto the bed and lifted my legs, jamming a pillow beneath my knees to keep them elevated. I could now add strong to my running list of her amazing attributes.

I heard water running again, but it sounded farther away this time. Mira was back a moment later and perched on the side of the bed. Her hands were gentle as she ran the cool cloth across the skin of my face and neck and readjusted the ice pack behind my head.

Her voice was just as soothing, her words not so much. "As soon as you're able, I'll help you get out of here. They won't hurt you here—again. Then you're on your own."

"I can't…go yet…" I mumbled.

"Even if you don't give a shit what happens to yourself, give a shit what happens to me, and stay away. This is under control. I don't need or want your help."

I tried hard to focus on her face. "I promised Sky."

Mira's eyes closed for a long moment before she met my gaze again. "You can't get justice for her if you're dead."

When I woke again, it was late or early—both really. No music, running water or low voices. It was quiet enough inside I could hear the occasional car drive by outside. Now was as good a time as any to make my move. Whatever had been decided about me, I really didn't want to be around to find out.

I raised my head. The ache was there, but the throbbing much improved. I was still dressed, even my boots and jacket. I patted my pockets and found I still had everything I came in with, which wasn't much. Shockingly, I still had my knife and ankle holster, weapon untouched. I couldn't imagine no one had checked to see if I was carrying when I was out of it. Just more likely they simply didn't consider me a threat, even armed. Bit of a blow to my confidence but I didn't have time to dwell. Let them underestimate me.

I stepped quietly past the curtains into the other room. There was just enough light to see Mira wasn't here. Do it, Lucky. Do it, now. I moved back through the tiny curtained-off bathroom and stepped up onto the bed. The books were partially covering a vent. That's how I could hear the other room so well even over the ringing in my ears. Is that what she had been looking at? Her ticket out was she'd overheard something that gave her leverage? I pushed the books carefully to each side away from the vent, right down the middle of the *Twilight* series and a small red light blinked back at me. What the hell? I tried to pull a book away but it was tethered by something—a thin black cord running from inside the vent to a hardback copy of *Eclipse*.

I picked up the book and something inside it shifted. It wasn't a book. It was hollow and opening it revealed a black, rubber encased device smaller than my hand. An external hard drive. Oh, shit. What was on the other end of that cord? A camera? A voice recorder? It didn't matter. I knew whatever was on it was going to be everything I needed to take down the Rat Lords. I unplugged it and jammed the device into my jacket pocket and jumped down, nearly landing on my ass when a wave of dizziness assaulted me, just as the door opened.

Mira came in and flicked on a small lamp. "You're up, good. Let's get you out of…" Her gaze swept me then trained on the wall above my head. Her expression turned from anxious to horrified. "What the hell?"

I looked back to see the books in disarray and the cord dangling empty. "This is it, Mira. We can—"

"What have you done?" she whispered and pushed me aside to see the hollow book empty.

I gripped her hand. "Let's go. While there's no one here."

She rounded on me, fists clenched. "There's always someone here."

Someone banged on the door. "Mira, you in there? I heard you up."

"Fuck, Boomer." I winced. "He lives here, too?"

"It's his place," she hissed. "Jesus Christ."

"Mira? You okay?" Boomer called.

She hurried to the door and said a little breathlessly, "Just a sec, baby. I'm not decent."

"You still have his bike keys?" I pocketed the handcuffs and keys—you never know—and moved everything else off the small end table onto the bed before pushing the table beneath the window.

"Yes, but I'm not leaving," she shout-whispered at me.

I put one foot up onto the table like I was preparing to step up and pulled my gun, leveling it at her. "You are. I need you to come with me."

Boomer pounded on the door and heavy thumping told me he was attempting to shoulder it open. "What the fuck, Mira? What's going on?"

Her glare was icy. "You're not going to shoot me, Lucky. Give me the hard drive. I'll still help you get out of here and cover for us both with Boomer."

She was right, I wasn't going to shoot her. I holstered the little gun and stepped up onto the table. "It's too late for that. You're coming with me."

"Like hell," she snarled.

I sighed, sorry not sorry for what I was about to do. "Boomer, can you hear me?"

"Don't!" Mira hissed.

"I can hear you, bitch!" he shouted back, followed by more shoulder thumping against the door. "If you hurt her, I'm gonna rip your goddamn arms off! Ain't no one around to protect you, now."

I banged open the window and opened it as far as it would go. It was far enough. "Thanks, but no thanks. Mira plays for my team. Didn't know? She's coming with me and all you motherfuckers are going to prison."

Boomer was quiet for several beats, apparently processing what I'd just said. Then he roared, "Callin' the boys and gettin' the goddamn keys! You're both dead!"

The color drained from Mira's face. "You have no idea what you've done."

That was probably true. I held out my hand. "We need to go. Now."

I slithered out the window and crashed down onto the gravel on my hands with my body following right behind. There was no time to assess any new pains. Mira had no choice but to follow me and I helped her down as much as I could, but she still hit the ground, just less hard. I offered her my hand.

"Back off." She smacked it away and popped up, sprinting around the side of the building like a college track star. I blinked and she was gone.

If I didn't move she was likely to leave me behind. Through the open window I heard the door crash open to her room. At least Boomer was at this end of the building now. I willed my weak body to run and heard the bike fire up as I rounded the corner to the front. She was already pulling away, but slowed just enough for me to slide on behind her. I wrapped my hands around her waist just in time not to be tossed off the back when she throttled away hard and we roared out of the parking lot. I turned back in time to see Boomer's shadowy bulk lumbering out the front door and then we were gone.

CHAPTER THIRTEEN

It was four in the morning and the roads were quiet which was ideal now that we were on the run. There was no being stealthy rumbling around on Boomer's Road King. We needed to get somewhere safe and figure out how I was going to get to my phone and call Angela. I didn't know what I had exactly, but I knew it was probably everything I needed to take down the club.

Mira drove the huge Harley with precision as she exited the highway that cut through downtown onto Broadway Avenue, weaving around potholes and broken asphalt. She slowed under the tangle of roads above us leading to the bridge that crossed the Hudson River into Troy. She stopped and parked beneath an overpass. The overpass where I'd last seen Skyler alive. Steep cracked concrete covered in graffiti led up underneath the onramp on either side of us. The engine ticked loudly with the cooling heat of our frantic escape.

The same tents and boxes were still there. Some were simply litter, others were homes. There was no movement, but I knew we were being watched.

Mira was off the bike and pulling items from one of the two enormous saddle bags. She tied her hair back loosely and slipped into a black zip-up sweatshirt and pulled up the hood. For the first time I realized how chilly it was. I was cold in my jacket and she was in nothing but ripped jeans and a thin T-shirt. She must have been freezing on that ride.

"Are you all right?" I asked and eased myself off the bike with a low groan.

She ignored my question. "They'll be able to track the bike. We're leaving it and the keys and with any luck it'll be gone within ten minutes. Give the club something to chase around for a while. It won't buy us much time, though."

"Listen, Mira, I'm sorry about what—"

"Shut up." She glared me to silence. "You have something I need, but before I add to your head injury and take it, we need to get somewhere safe and I need a secure phone."

I blinked stupidly at her. "Yeah, I have a phone. I just need to get—"

"No. Not yet." She grabbed me by the arm and dragged me down the street.

"Where are we going?" If it had been up to me, I would have driven us directly to the police station and kicked in Angela's office door while waving around the hard drive. It wasn't up to me—yet, and my breath came out raggedly as she set a fast pace and my body rebelled against all the physical activity so soon after my braining.

"Bus station," she said without slowing.

"I can't." I pulled her up short. "My phone and my contacts are here and—"

"How the hell did you ever become a cop? We're not getting it. You've jacked this up enough already for one night, and I need to see what I can salvage. Now, you're going to do what I say or you're going to get us killed. Period."

I needed her cooperation in addition to the hard drive so I let her pull me along again and muttered, "Come with me if you want to live."

"If only I had Sarah Connor on my team instead of you," she muttered back.

The bus station was quiet, save for a few people sleeping on cracked plastic benches, either homeless or waiting for an early morning connection, and a handful of staff.

Mira headed to the ticket counter and I followed dutifully, wondering how long I was going to let her be in charge. So far, she hadn't made any ridiculous decisions—unlike myself—so I was happy to let her lead the way for the moment if she had some plan in mind that would get us some place we could rest and regroup. She knew what we were up against better than anyone.

"The 4:50 to Plattsburg, has it left yet?" she asked the half-asleep attendant at the counter.

His head jerked up, and he peered out the window. "Nah, that's it in bay seven. You got a few minutes yet."

"Two tickets. One way."

"Yeah." He stabbed in some information into his computer. "Seventy-seven bucks."

Mira eyed me hard.

"What?"

"You see me have time to stop for cash?"

"Right." I peeled off a hundred-dollar bill.

Mira waggled her fingers at me. "Another."

I handed her another bill and she slid two hundred across the counter to the wide-eyed kid. "Anyone comes in looking for us, you make sure to tell them we got on that bus. Got it?"

His eyes never moved off the money. "Yeah, yeah. No problem, lady."

"Nice," I said. "Where'd you learn—"

"Save it," she snapped and grabbed my arm again, pulling me toward the restrooms.

Down a filthy hallway was a row of lockers in fairly decent repair. She crouched down to get at a bottom one with a commercial grade titanium padlock, which she apparently had the key for. She was just full of surprises. Whatever was in the locker was small enough for her to grab and jam in her back pocket without me seeing what it was.

"Let's go." She pulled her hood up again and headed back out to the street.

I wanted to ask again what her play was, but I figured she wouldn't answer me and so far I could work with what she had laid out. My energy was fading fast and I knew I'd have to save my strength for the confrontation we were heading toward. She was proving to be far more of a wild card than I'd anticipated and I didn't want her to get the upper hand. I still had control of the device, but I believed her when she said she was planning on taking it from me. Or trying to. I patted my pockets again, making sure I still had everything I needed to ensure that didn't happen.

Sunrise was just starting to color the horizon when we trudged into the parking lot of the U-shaped Downtown Motor Court Motel six blocks from the bus station. It looked exactly like the name suggested—cheap and shabby. There were a couple of beater cars in the lot along with two cabbies parked next to each other having coffee and a smoke.

I mindlessly headed to the office door but Mira steered me away and around back. There were rooms on this side, too, and if possible, it was even more decrepit. There was trash everywhere and it smelled like something, or someone, may have died back here. I covered my nose with my arm and tried not to gag.

"Let's go, princess." Mira pulled a key from her back pocket and unlocked a door before ushering me inside.

Was that key in the locker? Why would she have this? I was exhausted and my head was pounding again. Nothing was making sense anymore.

She flipped on the weak light and locked the door, pulling the chain across and making sure the curtains were drawn.

The room was surprisingly clean considering the outside. The bedspreads were dated and worn but unstained. There was very little dust and the carpet was neat. There was an old, solid radiator with chipped paint that I gave a quick once over, and the bathroom I poked my head in was small but scrubbed and nothing scurried away when I turned on the light. There were a couple threadbare but clean-looking towels and even a few individually wrapped soaps and plastic cups. Huh.

Mira leaned her back against the door and eyed me. "All right, Lucky. We're safe for the moment and playtime is over. Give me the device."

I held my hands out and smiled grimly. "I think I'm going to hang onto that, actually."

Mira smirked and started toward me slowly. "I don't know if you've looked at yourself in the mirror, but you are in no condition to take another beating. And make no mistake, I'm going to give you one if you don't hand over that hard drive. Now."

I jammed my hands into my back pockets and backed up as she approached. I just needed her a little closer. "But you do still think I'm cute, right?"

Mira's smirk vanished and I could see her tensing, readying to attack. "Lucky, I don't want to hurt you, but I will."

"Promise?"

Her left hand slammed into my chest and her right cocked back to deck me. Before she could take that swing I had a steel cuff around her left wrist and was jerking her to the floor. She dropped to her knees with a shout of surprise. When she realized what was happening she went for that right hook, which now had no power behind it and landed uselessly against my shoulder. I used her momentum to pull her further off-balance, threading the cuffs through the radiator pipe and locking the other bracelet around her right wrist. It was over in seconds.

She went wild-eyed and shuffled around on her knees. She pulled against the cuffs, the skin around her wrists bunching up and reddening. She grabbed the pipe to the radiator and jerked at it, trying to free it from the wall. "What the hell! Lucky, get these things off me."

With Mira secured now, albeit very angry, I felt like I could finally relax a little. I dropped heavily onto the end of the bed and let my aching head fall into my hands. "I'm sorry. I just need you to listen to me and not try and hurt me or get away until you understand what's going on."

"Woman, the only one in here who doesn't understand what's going on is you. Now get the fucking key and unlock me." Mira rattled the cuffs for emphasis.

"Stop doing that. You're going to hurt yourself." I pushed myself back to my feet and headed to the bathroom. I kept a wary eye on Mira, concerned she might try to trip me. She shuffled around again and sat down heavily, her back against the wall, the cuffs scraping against the radiator while she adjusted her position. Her breathing was hard and fast and her eyes blazed with fury. She was as angry as I'd ever seen anyone in my life.

I took her up on her suggestion to take a look at myself in the mirror. Yikes! There was dried flaking blood around my nose and mouth and a striped red abrasion across my left cheek that could actually be boot laces. Around the broken skin was light bruising and my left eye was slightly swollen.

I ran the water until it was warm and soaked a hand towel. I wiped my face and neck gently with soap and water to clean up. I unbuttoned my shirt and let it hang open while I ran the damp towel over my chest and beneath my bra, getting off the worst of the road grime. I could feel Mira's gaze on me, but when I looked over she had found some other place to focus her attention.

I unwrapped a plastic cup and guzzled two cups of water before filling it up again. I left my shirt open, making sure she got a good look when I offered her the water.

She arched a brow at me and jiggled the cuffs again, pinned down around the pipe at her side. "You gonna take these off?"

"No." I knelt down next to her and held the cup close to her lips.

"Go to hell," she muttered and turned away from me. "And if you think flashing your tits is going to endear me to you, you can fuck right the hell off."

"Fine." I slurped the water loudly and perched back on the end of the bed. "Let me tell you what's going on." I didn't wait for her to comment and plowed ahead. "I'm a cop. I mean not an *ex*-cop, an on-the-job cop, undercover. My real name is—"

"Detective Lucy Frances Sorin, Street Crimes Unit, badge number 1906, Albany PD."

I gaped at her. "What?"

"Your captain is Angela Curran, your partner is Ray Keller. Should I go on?"

"How do you know all this?"

"I'm ATF. And you're an idiot with a goddamn death wish."

I barked a laugh. "Yeah, right. You're ATF like Boomer's your dad."

"*My* real name is Special Agent Mira Van Allen. Keep the cover name close to avoid mistakes."

Oh my god. "I don't believe you. Why would you—"

"I've been undercover with the Rat Lords for over a year. More than a year of crawling around with this filth and you to come in and blow up my case in a matter of days."

I hid my uncertainty behind a smirk. "Sorry, who's been blowing what? Nice try."

She jerked upright as far as the cuffs would allow. "You think this is a joke? What I've had to do to get this deep?"

"Well, I'm certain there's a joke in there somewhere." I couldn't help the snort of laughter. I was really tired.

"Not one more fucking crack from you or—"

"Or what?" And really tired of her threats.

Her mouth thinned into a hard line, her expression all business. "All right, fine. If I'm just some back bar skank offering lap dances and smoking hog for a fiver how do I know Regulation 1976-6 is regarding tasers and firearms. 'Meaning any hand-held device designed to expel by means of an explosive two electrical contacts or barbs connected by two wires attached to a high voltage source in the device is classified as a firearm.'"

I crossed my arms. "Internet."

She laughed humorlessly and shook her head. "Seriously? Jesus, with shit instincts like yours I'm shocked you made it through the academy. And I suppose I would also have Googled Chapter 114 of Crimes and Criminal Procedure which covers trafficking in contraband cigarettes and smokeless tobacco. The term contraband cigarettes means a quantity in excess of 10,000 cigarettes—"

"Shut up for a second." Something was wrong. I could feel it. I buttoned my shirt. Shit instincts, my ass.

"Oh no, there's more."

"No, be quiet. I heard something." I stood in front of the door and leaned toward the window to part the curtain slightly and look left and right. I didn't see anything but an overflowing dumpster. I bent quickly to pull my weapon.

Mira's cuffs rattled again when she shifted back onto her knees. "Lucky, get these cuffs off me. You can't take them on yourself." The fear in her voice was real.

I dug in my pocket for the keys. If there was someone coming she deserved a chance to defend herself. I tossed the keys in her direction, unable to pay attention to where they landed. Sweat trickled down my neck and chest. "I think there's someone outside."

Two loud pops broke the silence. And the door. And my body. I spun from the door and crumpled onto the floor when an invisible force punched me in the gut and then poured invisible lava on me. White-hot pain streaked across my side just above my right hip and I could feel the warm, thick flow of blood soaking my jeans at the waist.

"Stay down!" Mira shouted as more bullets peppered the door for several seconds before it crashed in, sending splintering wood flying.

I'd never been shot before. I pressed one hand against the wound, afraid my hand was going to sink right into my belly and I'd be holding my own guts. That's not at all what happened. It hurt like hell, but I could manage. Maybe a graze. I looked around for my gun while Thor strode into the room, kicking it under the bed as soon as I reached for it. Then he kicked me in the side for good measure, sending me curling up into a ball of agony and the blood pouring anew.

"Griffin wants me to bring you back alive, Mira. He didn't say nothin' 'bout you being in one piece."

"You and what army?" Mira asked.

The calmness in her voice had me straining to move around so I could see her. I'm the one that got her here. I didn't think I could help against Thor, but the least I could do is bear witness to what happened next.

"Just me," Thor rumbled.

"That's what I wanted to hear." Mira let the cuffs drop to the floor and struck out a foot into his kneecap, snapping his leg back. She sprang into a crouch and punched him hard in the groin and then snapped her open palm into his nose when he doubled over.

He bellowed in pain and staggered backward, but she was on him in an instant, swinging around onto his back and locking her arms around his neck into a classic choke and hooking her legs around his hips so he couldn't dislodge her.

He choked and grunted, spinning around wildly for several long seconds until he dropped to his knees and finally onto his purpling face with his eyes rolling back up into his head.

Mira held him another moment before climbing off his back.

"Jesus," I gasped. "Is he dead?"

She checked his pulse. "No, but he won't be bothering us anytime soon."

She was all sweaty and disheveled and so sexy my head swam. Or maybe that was blood loss. "Where the hell did you learn that?"

She shot me a wicked glare. "ATF National Academy. Class of 2010."

CHAPTER FOURTEEN

"Ah, god." I flinched away from the pressure as Mira pressed a folded towel hard against my side.

"Hold this tight. I need to get us out of here and I can't have you dripping blood all over the place, giving us away. It's just a graze, but it's deep. Into the muscle."

"Yep, sure." I grunted and pushed myself up to sit against the foot of the bed. "No giving us away by bleeding to death. Got it."

Mira snorted. "You've lost a pint or two. Blood loss isn't the biggest concern. Infection is."

"How the hell did he find us?"

"That's a very good question. He didn't track the bike here. So, what did he track?" Mira sat back on her heels.

"You." I looked her over. "What has Hillis given you? A phone? Jewelry?"

Mira shook her head, her lips pursed. "Nothing."

"Something. Think, Mira. Clothes? Anything that you're wearing?"

She paused and looked down at herself. "He…he…won me this belt buckle at a rally shortly after we met. But he would have had to arrange it in advance."

We both stared at the chrome mud flap girl. Mira whipped the belt off and turned over the buckle, smoothing her fingers over the back. "I don't know. I can't see anything." She held it up and looked at it from the side. "Shit."

I cocked my head to see it from the angle she was looking. "It's thicker in the middle."

"It's been altered and soldered. I never noticed. I mean it just looked like the normal crap metalwork on this kind of freebie. There's enough room for a microchip and battery. Griffin liked me to wear it. That bastard chipped me. He's been tracking me this whole time."

"Does that mean you've been made? Does he know who you are?"

"No, he never would have let it get this far if he knew who I was. I lived the life. I never had secret meetings with my handler. Everything was out in the open. My information was handed over through the salon where I got my hair and nails done. Darcy, my handler, went under as an employee six months before me. Griffin loved it when I got my hair and nails done. He gave me a ride most of the time. My operation was airtight."

"Until I blew it up." I sighed wearily.

Mira jerked the lamp out of the wall and prepared to smash it into the buckle. "Does this mean you believe me, now?"

I raised my hand and stretched to cover the buckle. "Jesus, yes, I believe you, Agent Van Allen. Don't smash it. We can use it and send them off again."

She considered a moment and then lowered the lamp. "Right. Okay. Let me think. They can track Thor's bike, so we need to get that out of here, too." She crawled over to him and started going through his pockets.

"And maybe…his phone," I slurred and felt myself starting to tip over. Now that the immediate danger had passed and I wasn't going to die right away, the adrenaline keeping me upright seeped away, leaving me weak and shaky.

"Oh, Christ, not again." Mira propped me back up and pulled the towel away to check the wound in my side. "Didn't realize you Street Crimes folks were so fragile. You're still bleeding. Press harder." She placed both of my hands over the towel.

"I don't think I can...help you...with..." My head bobbed.

"I need to get you somewhere safe. I don't know how long I'm gonna be and they'll come looking for Thor eventually. They may be on their way here now."

I could only watch her now and barely even that. She blurred in and out and every time I blinked she was in a different part of the room. She could teleport, too. Dope.

"What about this is funny to you?" she asked.

"What?" Had I been laughing?

"Forget it. You're a mess." She got an arm around my back and hoisted me to my feet.

My cry of pain was hoarse and pathetic even to my own ears.

"Suck it up, Street Crimes, and hold that towel tight. No drips, remember. We're not going far."

She staggered us out of the room and down the back of the building. She toed open the door to another room exactly like the one we just left. Or was it the same room? But when did she have time to clean? God, I loved this woman.

Oh, god, the bed was so soft and I was so tired. Maybe just a little nap...

Ow! Something pulled at the wound. It burned and ached. I tried to roll away but a strong hand on my hip kept me still.

"Don't move."

God. Jesus. What the fuck was she doing to me? I tried to bring my right hand up to push her away, but it just rattled up by my head, metal biting into my wrist. My left arm flopped over and groped along my side.

She pushed my hand away. "Stop it. I'm almost done."

Done what? I managed to drag my eyes open. She was bent over me, pushing a hooked needle through my skin. Repeatedly. I rolled my head to the right. I was handcuffed to the headboard. There was an IV tube taped to the back of my right hand and the bag it attached to hung from the light fixture on the wall above my head.

My head felt like a balloon and my tongue was two sizes too big for my mouth. "What did…you give me?"

"Normal saline to keep your blood pressure up, antibiotics to combat infection, and a splash of morphine to get you through this part."

"Which part?" I looked down. I was laying on bloodstained towels, naked but for my bra and underwear. Wrappers and bloody gauze littered the floor. The wound in my side, which I never really got a good look at in all its glory, was now a neatly stitched line about six inches long, surrounded by swollen skin.

"This part." She emptied a bottle of alcohol over me.

"Aw, fuck!" I hissed and jerked away, panting against the burn. "Jesus Christ."

"Someone has never been shot and treated in the field before and it shows."

I gritted my teeth and breathed through my nose until the worst of it passed. "And you have?"

"Twice." She started bagging up the trash. "I can't give you anything more for pain because of your likely concussion."

"You an undercover doctor, too?" Please, say yes.

"Just advanced training in tactical field medicine."

Close enough. "And the cuffs?"

"I knew I'd be gone for a while and I didn't want you waking up and trying something dumb."

"And they're still on because?"

She dropped back into the chair next to me and ripped open several sterile bandages and a roll of medical tape.

She squeezed half a tube of antibiotic ointment over the wound and pressed a thick bandage over it, securing it with tape across my belly and around my side. "I like you better like this."

"Handcuffed to a bed naked? You really are a kinkster. Guess your cover wasn't much of a stretch after all."

She sighed. "Out of my way and out of danger, so you can't fuck this up worse than you already have. Listen, my field training never covered subcutaneous sutures, which you need.

You move around too much, you're going to open that wound back up and we're going to have a problem."

"And by *we* you mean me." I shifted on the bed and felt the sharp sting and pull of the sutures. It really hurt.

"Yeah, well, as much as I'd like to leave your reckless ass here and get back to my team, we're in this together now. Whether I like it or not. And just to be clear, I do not like it at all."

"Yeah, I got that," I said wearily. The stress and pain were taking their toll and my emotions were in overdrive—fear, anger, and guilt all battling for attention. My eyes burned with fatigue and unshed tears. "Can't we just take a cab down to your office or something?"

She stared at me, shaking her head. "I'm going to chalk that bit of idiocy up to blood loss. We can't bring the shitstorm that we're in right now down to the government district. Better we stay here and let help come to us. As long as the club thinks they still have a chance to contain this—us—then they won't go to ground. As soon as I go in, they'll scatter and torch everything and everyone along the way. I'm not willing to take that chance. We can still make our case and minimize the collateral damage."

"Right, okay." I was so out of my league, right now, on so many different levels.

Mira studied me, but I couldn't look at her. She shifted in her chair. "Here, I thought you might want this."

I rolled my eyes to her extended hand. I rattled my cuffed right wrist and glared at her until she leaned across me, so I could take whatever she had with my left. I expected ibuprofen, but she dropped a gold chain with an *S* pendant into my hand. Skyler's necklace from her sister.

The gold chain was warm from being near Mira's body. Grief and guilt took over from fear at the sight of it. "Why do you have this?" I breathed, the tears I was battling against so fiercely began to fall as I was reminded of all the promises I made to Skyler. And what I had put her through as a condition of my promised help.

"I didn't have it until recently. Shade did."

My muddled brain allowed a piece to click into place. "That's what you were arguing about in the bathroom."

"That's right."

I frowned. "But she wouldn't give it to you."

Mira shrugged one shoulder. "I called in a favor. There's a club member with very sticky fingers."

I nodded. "Did Shade kill Sky?"

Mira closed her eyes for a long moment before meeting my gaze. "Yes. I'm sorry."

Anger pushed grief out of the way. "And you knew Shade was going to kill her?"

Mira pressed her lips together and looked away. That was answer enough and my rage flared, adrenaline surging through me and I lunged out of bed—or tried to.

Mira easily blocked my weak left arm as I swung at her. "No," she said simply and pressed me back against the bed. "That won't help and you'll start bleeding again."

I panted in fury and pain. "Why didn't you do something? You're a goddamn cop!"

"So are you," she said softly.

She didn't say the rest of the sentence. She didn't have to. I shuddered. Why didn't I do something? Why didn't I go after Sky that day on the bridge? Why didn't I look for her again before the raid? Why didn't I pull her out the second she gave me the address? Why? Why? Why?

I swallowed hard and stared at the ceiling. If I could have turned away from her to hide my shame I would have. I covered my face with my left hand, the necklace tangled between my fingers and the pendant resting against my lips as the tears fell relentlessly. It must be the morphine. A whoosh of air above me had me opening my eyes when Mira covered me with a sheet from the other bed.

She cleared her throat, a sign she was warring with emotions of her own. "You want to know where we stand?"

"Yeah." My voice cracked and I knuckled my face dry. "Can I get some water?"

She produced a thick green smoothie with a straw and held it while I got my left hand around it. "Drink as much as you can.

It's kale and grapefruit, and other stuff. The nutrients will help with red blood cell production."

I sucked on it and grimaced. "It's awful."

"I'm aware. Drink more."

She was close, watching me while I drunkenly slurped up a seaweed smoothie. I noticed for the first time she was freshly showered. Her hair was damp and skin makeup free. She was in clean clothes. A black long-sleeve T-shirt, olive cargo pants, plain black belt and black boots. She looked ready to lead an incursion at the Gap.

"I got you some clothes, too." She nodded to the chair by the door.

"Thanks." I gave up on the smoothie. Sucking through a straw was suddenly exhausting.

"It's okay if you need to rest," she said as if reading my mind, or more likely my probable colorless complexion and drooping eyes. "You've had a rough couple of days."

I frowned and tried to see out the window, but the curtains were tightly drawn. "Is it night again?"

"Pretty much." She sat back in the chair and placed the drink on the nightstand. "I got rid of Thor's bike, which was easy enough. Tucked his phone and the belt buckle into a saddle bag. Borrowed a white coat and badge from a residents' room and took a walk through Albany Med to pick up some supplies. And then went shopping. With your money, by the way."

"Now what?" I was having trouble keeping my eyes open.

"Now we sit tight and wait for the cavalry."

"Who?"

"I called the salon and got a message to my handler. She's going to let my team know we need urgent extraction. They'll get in touch with your team and read them in. I will admit if we had been collaborating with your department, we might not be where we are right now. I don't know why we weren't. My people should be here in a couple hours. I told them we were safe enough for now. I heard bikes come and go a few hours ago, collecting Thor. They didn't think to look for us four doors down and I wouldn't have expected them to. Total baller move making the same hotel the second extraction location.

My team's sending agents out to get eyes on the club members and surveilling Boomer's to make sure they know where the bad guys are before they come and collect us."

"Okay, good." Wait. Not good. Get in touch with *my* team? It was like a shot of adrenaline to my heart and my eyes flew open, my heart banging in my chest.

Mira sat up. "What's wrong?"

"Someone on my team is on the take," I blurted.

"What? What are you saying?"

"I'm saying, Curran thinks there's a mole in my unit...wait, no, a *rat* in my unit," I babbled as clearly as I could. I was having a hard time knowing if I was making sense.

"How...Why didn't you say—"

"Can we discuss this later? Unlock me. We have to get out of here."

She had the keys in her hand before I'd finished speaking. Once the cuffs were off, I sat up quickly and nearly threw up for my trouble. "Oh, shit," I groaned, swallowing heavily while my stomach turned inside out. There was less pain than I expected. Guess the morphine was still doing its thing. I ripped the IV from the back of my hand.

"Go slow." She set clean clothes next to me on the bed.

"We don't have time for slow." I pulled on navy joggers, loose white T-shirt and a matching navy zip-up hoodie. All a little baggy, but not falling off.

"Sorry." Mira looked me over. "I thought you'd be headed straight to the hospital and would appreciate something comfortable. "I got you cool kicks, though." She held up a pair of black slip-on Vans.

"It's fine. There are pockets." I jammed my feet in the shoes, grateful I didn't have to bend over to tie laces. I emptied the pockets of my trashed jeans of what money we had left and my knife, stashing them in the sweats. We still had several hundred dollars, so we'd be fine in the short term. My weapon, which Mira must have collected, went back on my right leg and I nearly fell over in the process. Head rush.

Mira slipped on a black nylon pancake holster with a compact 9mm Sig Sauer onto her belt and slid it around to her back. Where the hell did she get that? She threw on her black hoodie to cover it and started cramming what few supplies we had into a black backpack, including the external hard drive.

No need to find my jacket. I was plenty warm enough and now I knew it was empty. "Got everything?" I asked, eyeing the backpack.

"Yeah." She looked at it, too, then handed it over. "Hold on to this? I'll be driving."

"Sure." Was that trust we just exchanged? I was so giddy at the thought I started to whip the backpack over my shoulders and immediately doubled over, gripping my hip. "Ah, fuck."

She let the perfect opportunity to mock my condition slide and helped me into the straps instead. "Thanks."

"You wreck my awesome patch job and I'll have your ass," she said wryly and headed cautiously out the door.

"I'll just bet you will," I muttered and followed her out. It was dusk, the sun low in the sky, casting long shadows over everything. Hopefully if they were sending someone to finish the job they would wait until dark and give us a few more minutes.

Mira was pulling on a helmet and swinging her leg over a beat-up Yamaha that looked like it had seen more than its fair share of adventures. She handed me a helmet.

"Where you'd get this?" I crammed the helmet on and secured the chin strap.

"Traded a kid on the street for it." She kick-started it and revved the throttle.

"Traded what? Oh, right. Thor's bike. That makes sense." I pulled the straps of the backpack snug and climbed on behind her. This time she waited for me to settle comfortably and wrap my arms around her waist before taking off. That was progress, I think.

CHAPTER FIFTEEN

Mira drove just as skillfully on this small, ratty bike as she had on the Harley. I could tell she was doing her best to avoid the rough patches, but we were wending our way through some of the poorest neighborhoods with the worst roads. Every bump and pothole had me gritting my teeth. No doubt she was aware of my discomfort with how hard I was holding on to her. It was agony.

It was nearing eight at night and the sun was just setting. It was still busy out on every corner with people coming in and out of every downtown deli, cafe, pub, and convenience store. We stuck to neighborhood roads and even ducked down some alleyways running behind low stretches of brownstone apartments.

She turned down another alley and we puttered along between rusted chain-link fences surrounding postage stamp backyards, overgrown with grass and weeds. She weaved us around busted trash cans and broken bicycles and came to a stop outside a fence in marginally better shape than the others.

"We're here." She took off her helmet and shook out her hair, but remained seated. "Go ahead."

I shifted my grip to her shoulders and used her to steady myself to get off, staggering slightly when my legs were forced to take my full weight again. I took off my helmet and scratched my itchy scalp. I hadn't gotten a shower yet.

She hopped off and eyed me. "You all right?"

"Yeah. Just sore."

"Show me." She reached for the zipper on my sweatshirt.

I knocked her hand away. "It's fine."

She pinned me with a look. "Let's not do this, okay? Someone or more likely several someones are trying to kill us. I need to know if I can count on you to have my back."

I held her gaze and unzipped my sweatshirt. I already knew what she was going to see. I could tell I was bleeding again ten minutes into the drive over. I knew the shirt was soaked through over the bandage.

"Jesus. Okay. I'll take a look again when we get inside. I'll try packing the wound and stitching you back together again. That should stop the bleeding until we can get paramedics. Hopefully, soon." She unlatched the gate.

"Whose house is this?" I followed behind.

"ATF rented the place at the beginning of the op. I worked out of here while we ran up intelligence analysis and laid the groundwork for my cover. That was six months' worth of work before I even went under."

I grunted. "Yeah, I got it. I fucked up."

She turned, her brow furrowed. "That's not what I meant."

Whatever. "Who uses it now?"

"Special Agent Darcy Minor, my friend, handler, and the best damn manicurist this side of the Hudson." She wiggled her French tips at me.

"Very nice. But you're gonna have to cut those."

She rolled her eyes, but couldn't hide her smile. "You're a piece of work."

My grin faded when I looked past her to the house. "The door's open."

"What?" Mira spun around to see where I was looking and drew her weapon from her back.

I crouched to pull mine from my ankle and gasped in pain. "Shit." I could barely stand back up. Note to self, keep it in your pocket.

"Stay behind me." Mira held her sidearm close to her body and turned sideways, making her a smaller target as she moved smoothly up the back porch stairs.

I followed right behind her as she stepped into the kitchen. Not clean and scrubbed like the house where we found Sky, but lived in and messy. There was an old cup of coffee on the small kitchen table, dishes in the sink, and a pot of soup on the stove. Mira hovered her hand over the stove then brought it down silently on top, letting me know it was cool.

She moved forward into the dining room. A half-finished bowl of soup sat at the single place setting at the dining room table. Either someone was interrupted or was simply not a neat freak. Given what I'd seen so far, I wanted it to be the latter, but my heart raced knowing there had been trouble here. My gaze darted left and right; I knew how to clear a house. She went through to the living room and I broke off down the hallway to the right to an office with wraparound desk and state-of-the-art tech—all upended and smashed—but clear of threats. The bathroom on this level was clear. No bodies in the tub.

We met back at the foot of the stairs leading up.

She gestured toward the back of the house and mouthed "basement" before heading upstairs. I headed back toward the kitchen. We must have passed the basement door on the way in.

The basement door was partially hidden behind the open back door. We walked right by it. A dustpan and broom hung on the outside. It was closed tightly but didn't appear to have a lock on it. A thump on the floor above me and unintelligible shout from Mira tore my attention from the door.

"Mira, you okay?" I called and stepped away from the basement door just far enough to avoid getting brained again when it crashed open and a man hurtled out, slamming into me and driving us both into the back door. My right shoulder smashed out the glass window, but I managed to hold on to my gun. He was too close to me to get off a shot, but I brought the butt down hard on the back of his head. Once. Twice. The third time he cried out and pushed me away. Right into the corner of the counter. Fuck me.

I could hear Mira thundering down the stairs but not fast enough. It was Slug and he was coming at me again with a snarl. I fired off two rounds. The first one missed and the second clipped him in the arm, spinning him out of the way of my third shot which splintered a cabinet behind his head.

We were so close together in the small kitchen my gun was practically useless. He lashed out with his foot, catching me behind the knee, not hard but enough to stagger me and grab my wrist, jerking the gun from my hand. It clattered even more uselessly to the floor. Motherfucker just disarmed me. With an Amazonian battle cry I threw a wild punch with my left and connected solidly with his face, breaking his nose—and possibly my hand—in an explosion of blood and snot.

"Hold it, Slug," Mira barked, weapon pointed at his head.

He fell to his knees, eyes streaming tears and blood pouring through his fingers covering his face. "You bitches are fucking dead," he whined.

I collected my gun from the floor and straightened with effort and a lot of heavy breathing. I engaged the safety and dropped it into my left pants pocket. My right hand was too busy pressing into my hip to try and stem my own blood, which was flowing freely now after that fight. "By the way, shithead. You didn't beat me. I let you win that game. Loser." I grabbed the pot off the stove and bashed him in the side of the head with a spray of chicken noodle. He went down without a twitch.

"You all right?" Mira holstered her weapon at the small of her back, her gaze sweeping me up and down.

"Great, yeah." I leaned heavily against the counter and pulled my hand away to show it covered in blood.

Her mouth quirked up. "That was very un-Krav Maga-like. Where'd you learn to throw a haymaker like that?"

"School of hard knocks." I flexed my hand. Not broken but sore as hell. "Your contact here? Agent Minor, is she…?"

Mira's mouth twisted around in what I recognized as an effort not to cry. She cleared her throat. "She's upstairs. They were here a while. I'm sure they wanted any information they could get out of her. Probably not much. She was tough as hell."

"Shit. I'm so sorry, Mira." I didn't know what else to say. Murdering assholes. This was totally out of control. An ATF agent was dead. "You think there was more than one?"

"I'm certain of it." She gestured to Slug, unconscious on the floor. "This dropout never could've taken her on his own. They probably just left him here to see if anyone else turned up and we bumbled into him."

"How did they find this place?"

She shrugged. "The salon was the only place I ever went without being watched. Would've been pretty easy to track Darcy down once they knew to take a closer look at my movements."

"Or the Rat on my team…" I trailed off, sick to my stomach that her friend was dead, and my actions or bad seeds in my unit were directly responsible.

"Or that," she said flatly.

"What are you gonna do?"

She shook her head. "I don't know. I need to think. I haven't slept in two days and you need—"

"I'm fine," I lied and started pulling open drawers until I found a stack of clean dish towels. That'll do. I grabbed two. A few more drawers later I had a roll of duct tape. I unzipped my sweatshirt and pulled up my shirt. Blood flowed freely in a stream from the middle of the wound where the stitches had broken. I pressed the folded towels against my side and ripped the tape with my teeth.

"All right, Street Crimes, you've convinced me. You're a badass." She knelt in front of me and took the tape, securing the towels over the wound and wrapping the tape around my waist several times. "How's that?"

"Tight." I winced.

"Good. Someone will have called in those shots by now. Add whatever food and medical supplies you can to that backpack. Check the bathroom, too. No electronics. Nothing that can track us. I'll be right back. We're gone again in two minutes," she called, disappearing back upstairs.

I bagged the rest of the towels and the tape. In the same junk drawer was a pocketknife with a bunch of features, a lighter, and a roll of twine. Who was I, fucking MacGyver? I also grabbed a small flat pry bar. I had no idea what I would use it for, but at the very least I could defend myself with it if I needed to.

I didn't fare much better with the food, but collected a box of granola bars, bottles of water and juice, a plastic container of what looked like chicken pasta salad, plastic forks, and a bottle of wine. In the bathroom I added more medical tape, an elastic bandage, some gauze, bottle of alcohol, Band-Aids, and bottle of ibuprofen.

"Time's up, let's go!" Mira shouted from the kitchen.

She was already heading out the back door with a stuffed gray duffel over her shoulder. I followed her out into the dark and headed for the bike.

"Leave that. You can't ride it." She headed down the alley the opposite way and stopped at a small garage, unlocking it with a key she must have taken from her friend. She raised the door.

"Whoa, sweet," I whispered, goggling at the matte black Ford Mustang.

"It's just our unmarked."

"This is government issue? I thought you said don't take anything they can track?"

"We're not keeping it. I just want to get as far away from this house right now as we can. And I need to call this into my team. We need a new car and I need a burner phone."

"Lucky?" A shadow emerged from the backyard into the alleyway.

Mira pulled her weapon lightning fast.

"Whoa, whoa." I stepped in front of her. "Ray? What are you doing here?"

"Hands where I can see them," Mira barked and moved out from behind me, making sure I wasn't in her line of fire. "Step forward into the light."

Ray raised his hands and moved slowly into the weak back porch light from a nearby house. "Lucky, what the hell is going on?"

He looked like shit, more unkempt and unshaven than usual. His eyes were red-rimmed and he'd lost weight. I watched him warily. "How are you here, Ray?"

He stepped closer, his brow furrowing as he looked me over. He reached out. "Jesus, Lucky, are you—"

"Stay where you are!" Mira said dangerously.

He backed up, watching her nervously. "You're Agent Van Allen? What's happening?"

"Answer the question. What are you doing here, Keller?" Mira said tightly.

"We got briefed on ATF's operation a few hours ago. We went to the motel with your team to extract you, but you were gone. The place was trashed and there was blood—"

"Who briefed you?" Mira asked.

"Um, Agent…uh…Agent Dennison," he stammered. "Can you lower your weapon, please, Agent Van Allen?"

"No. Who took the original call from Dennison?" Mira demanded.

"What? I don't know. Not me. The whole team was briefed," he said angrily. "What's going on. Lucky, please. Where have you been? Are you all right?"

"What are you doing here, Ray. Right here, right now?" I asked, panicked and paranoid. Please, not Ray. Not Ray. I could hear distant sirens. Wow, the response time here was shit.

"When you weren't at the motel, ATF checked in with their agent here, Agent Minor. She said she hadn't been contacted since she first heard from Agent Van Allen earlier this evening."

I motioned for him to go on. "And?"

"And I got worried. We didn't have eyes on you, there was blood…I went to your apartment. The door had been kicked off the hinges and your place all torn up. I just thought I'd come out and talk with her and see if there was something I could do."

"Without backup?" Mira said.

He glared at her, his face reddening. "Lucky is my fucking backup, lady. She's my partner and I want to know what the hell is going on."

"Curran thinks there's a mole in the department. Someone on the Rat Lords' payroll," I blurted.

He gaped at me. "What? Who?"

I stared at him. Mira cocked her gun. The sirens were getting louder.

His eyes went wide. "Me? You think it's me? Lucky, come on."

"You're here and Darcy Minor, *my* partner, is dead—after being tortured for information. There was a club member waiting for us in the basement," Mira said icily.

Ray's head whipped around to the house and back to us. "I wasn't here. I never went in. I went to the front door. No one answered so I came around back and heard you. I swear to Christ, Lucky, I'm on your side. Always."

I exhaled loudly, the fight going out of me. "Jesus, Ray, I'm—"

A shot pinged off the cement at Mira's feet. She spun away and cried out, a hand going to her cheek.

"Shit!" Ray shouted and dove behind some overturned trash bins.

"Mira!" I moved toward her, fighting my baggy sweatpants pockets for my weapon as more shots popped off, cracking into the cement and splintering the side of the garage. One shot close enough to my head I heard the whizz.

Mira screamed, "Get in the car!"

She didn't need to tell me twice. I'd already been shot once today—or was that yesterday? I dove into the Mustang's passenger seat while she jumped behind the wheel. The Mustang rumbled to life and we roared out of the alley, my heart hammering so hard and my hands shaking. I never saw what happened to Ray, but I knew he wasn't the one shooting at us.

CHAPTER SIXTEEN

If Mira was as rattled as I was, she didn't show it. Her hands were relaxed on the wheel and her face was expressionless and pale except for the blood oozing down her cheek from the ricochet. It didn't look too deep but still needed to be cleaned and bandaged.

I couldn't stand the silence but I didn't know what to say.

"Your partner set us up," she said coolly.

"What? No. I don't believe that."

"I don't care what you believe. My partner is dead and yours is on the take."

She whipped down a side street and slammed on the brakes, sending me jerking against the seat belt with a shriek of pain. "Fuck, Mira!" I clutched at my side, pressing down hard on the tape and towels.

"Get out," she spat. "You're on your own. We're done here."

"There's no way. Not Ray."

"He was armed. Why didn't he return fire?"

"Why didn't *you*? I didn't see a shooter. Did you? We were in the middle of a densely populated neighborhood. He took cover, same as us."

"He stalled us there. Set us up to be ambushed."

I shook my head, gritting my teeth. "I'm sorry about Darcy. I'm sorry about your case. I'm sorry about *my* case. I'm sorry I couldn't help Sky. I'm sorry I'm not Sarah Connor. I'm fucking sorry about a lot of things, but it's not Ray. Those shots were meant to kill us. If Ray is in on it, why didn't he just shoot us in the back when he had the chance? He totally had the advantage and approached, weapon holstered. To talk."

"He wanted to find out what we know." There was less conviction behind her words now and she turned toward me.

"He answered *our* questions. The only thing he *asked* was if I was all right. I trust him."

"I don't."

"Then trust *me*." I forced my brain into overdrive to try and find a way out of this. "Can we go into the field office?"

"Even if we made it there, they'd probably shoot us on sight if we just roll up looking like this, and no doubt the ATF is being watched by now. We'll be dead before we make it to the front door." She shook her head. "I need to make contact with my team and get a secure extract location."

"Then contact them."

"On what? My shoe phone?" She stared at me hard, clearly wrestling against all the same emotions I was: anger, fear, and grief. "I'm just so goddamn tired," she whispered.

I reached for her hand, covering hers with my own. "I know. I am, too. But we need to keep going. Let's ditch the car then and get somewhere safe where we can rest."

She stared at our hands for a long moment, finally turning her hand over to lace her fingers with mine, squeezing gently. "I think I do trust you, Lucky," she said softly.

"Thank you," I replied just as softly.

She released my hand and gunned the car down the street. "Though I'm not sure I believe the name *Lucky* suits you so well."

"No shit."

I sighed and tipped my head back against the seat, fatigue and injury weighing me down. I couldn't imagine how exhausted Mira must be. I got some sleep last night and I slept part of today. Was that only today? My mind was playing funny tricks on me. I could have sworn it was a week ago.

I blinked and we were parked underground and Mira wasn't in the car or anywhere I could see. I had both of our bags in my lap and the Mustang engine was still ticking like it hadn't been shut down for long. A sign on the column in front of me said Empire State Plaza. We must be in the lot beneath the Convention Center.

A car pulled in next to me and parked. Mira jumped out and flung my door open before I even had a chance to panic.

"Let's go." She lifted the bags from me and helped me out of the car.

"Where'd you get this?" I asked as I climbed in the passenger side of the very uninteresting gray Camry.

"Borrowed it." She backed us out and headed to the exit. "I need to stop for a phone."

Shoot your shot, Sorin. She's been leading the charge from the jump. Very capably and you'd be dead several times over without her, but still. Are you going to just sit here or are you going to take back your damn case, find the mole, bring down the Rat Lords, get justice for Sky and maybe along the way show Special Agent Mira Van Allen that you're good for something besides practice for her tactical medical skills? And maybe prove to Angela you are worthy of that gold shield that's so important to you. Do it. Do it now. And for fuck's sake sound like you know what you're doing. "We need to get *my* phone. It's a burner dedicated for my extract."

"I suppose you're going to tell me the person at the other end couldn't possibly be involved, too, right?"

"That's right. Captain Angela Curran gave it to me when she gave me this assignment." I went on before she had a chance to come up with an argument. "Head over to Capitol Crossfit. You know where it is?"

"Off 9W by the Thruway entrance?"

"That's it, yeah. There's a cheap hotel there, too. We can regroup and get some rest. Make the call from there."

Mira was quiet a long time, staring straight out the windshield, but she was heading in the right direction.

She parked among other cars but not right next to anyone and we had a clear line of sight to the entrance. It was after nine now and the gym closed at eleven. Most people were coming out and few were going in.

After several minutes, Mira broke the silence. "If they've trashed your place, they're all up in your life now. Beanie is pretty slick with computers. He handles the vetting for new members. Pretty deep background checks."

I snorted. "So, something like having not one, but two undercover cops infiltrate the club doesn't happen?"

"That's right. My team took the better part of a year to prep this op. Whatever you did to set up your cover must've been tight."

"Got my CI killed, botched a raid, smacked a superior and got fired," I said dryly.

"I can't speak to the rest of it, but what happened to Sky wasn't any more your fault than it was mine."

"Or, as much your fault as it was mine," I countered.

"That, too. My point is, they'll know about this place."

"Yeah, I thought about that at the beginning. I actually assumed someone from the club would come snooping around my apartment a lot sooner. I'm not an official member here. Not on paper. I'm sort of Angela's occasional plus one. I have a guest pass and use her locker. I don't even keep the key card on me. It's stashed between the far-right mirror over the sink. It pulls away a bit from the wall."

"Weird, but okay."

Was that approval? Point to me. I opened the door but she was quick to grab me by the arm and pull me back in.

"I don't think so. You can't go in there like that." She gestured to my blood-soaked clothes. "I got it. What's the locker number?"

"Uh, twenty-three, but you're bleeding, too."

She leaned up to see herself in the rearview mirror and prodded her cheek. It had stopped bleeding, but looked a mess. "Damn."

"Here, I got it." I rummaged through my supplies, my hand falling comfortingly onto the hard drive, the only thing making any of this worth it, before grabbing up the gauze, alcohol, and bandages. I soaked gauze in alcohol and cupped her chin in my hand. "Turn toward me. Ready?"

"Go."

As gently as I could, I cleansed the wound and cleared the blood from her face, but the tightness around her mouth gave away her discomfort. It had started bleeding again. I pressed a gauze pad to the one-inch laceration. "Hold this." It was deeper than I thought and could use some stitches—and a professional hand. The best I could do was three small Band-Aids. At least they were good quality. I lined them up neatly, pulling the skin together tightly to close the wound. "How's that?"

She checked herself in the mirror and nodded again. "Good work. Maybe there's hope for you yet."

"All right, go. Hurry up before it bleeds through."

She made no move to get out of the car. Her mouth pressed into a hard line when she looked at me intensely. "Do you trust me, Lucky?"

"I...I mean, you've saved my life. Even after I essentially kidnapped you. You've kept us both out of Rat Lords' hands, and you didn't shoot Ray."

"Do. You. Trust. Me?"

I didn't know. I'd known her what, one week, ten days maybe? But only a couple of days as law enforcement. I had no idea who she was or what she was capable of. Or did I? She was strong, smart, clever, and resourceful. She could fight. She didn't kill, but I had no doubt she would if she had to. She cared about people. She was thoughtful, considerate, and could recognize when she might be wrong. She trusted me, or at least said she did. After carrying us this far didn't I at least owe her the same in return?

"I trust you, Mira," I said and meant it.

She nodded slowly. "Good. I promise you, your trust in me is not misplaced. Whatever happens next, remember that." She grabbed up the gray duffel she brought from the house and was out the door.

"What does that mean?" I called after her, but she was gone.

She disappeared into the gym for a long time. Way longer than it should have taken to get to the locker room and back. My nerves jangled as I watched the door intently, every couple of minutes scanning the parking lot for threats and keeping my ears tuned for the tell-tale rumble of Harleys. And there it was. Shit. The unmistakable engine noise grew louder and I sank down in the seat, gripping my weapon hard while it slowly cruised the parking lot right behind the car. My heart hammered as the driver of a black Fat Boy turned down the aisle in front of me and parked.

A man unzipped his leather jacket and straightened his tie. Wait. What? I inched my way up in the seat as he removed his helmet and finger-combed his trendy hair. When he checked his teeth in the sideview mirror I let out a loud breath and unclenched my…everything. Jesus. He headed to the bar next to the gym.

My heart rate had just returned to normal when a red Dodge Caravan pulled up right next to me, blocking my view of the gym and my first reaction was annoyance. The driver pressed his face against the window and sneered. It was Phil Lyons and fear spiked through me. Neal leaned forward from the passenger seat and waggled his fingers my way. Why were they in a goddamn minivan? If they weren't on patrol, this likely wasn't an official stop and not looking good for me.

Adrenaline surged, urging me to action. I couldn't let them take me in, but I wasn't sure I could fight them either. Even if I could take them both right now in the middle of a busy shopping center, was I going to take off with Mira inside? Shit. Even if Lyons and Neal weren't involved, whoever was would have a clear shot at me and the evidence, if I was in custody. I grabbed the device from the backpack and tucked it under the seat. Best I could do on short notice. I dug out the small utility knife I'd taken from the house. They would search me. I lifted my shirt, and jammed it between the bloody towels and my skin. Fuck me, that hurt.

The passenger door jerked open and Neal stuck his punk head in, his right hand on his service weapon. But he wasn't in uniform.

"Where ya been, Sorin?" He pulled me out by the arm. "We been lookin' everywhere for you."

"I'll search the car," Lyons announced.

"Hey, boys." I tried to be cool, but I was in absolute panic mode and was certain I was going to stroke out any second.

Neal pushed me toward the back and shoved me up against the trunk, kicking my legs apart, keeping one hand in the middle of my back. He pulled my gun and auto knife from my pockets but the necklace was too small for him to notice. There went the rest of my cash, too. He ran his hand over the bulge of bandages on my right hip.

"What the hell?" He jerked his bloody hand away and wiped it across my back. "Nasty. What the hell happened to you?"

"I got shot."

"No kidding?" The handcuffs clinked as he pulled them free. "What was that like?"

This was going from bad to worse fast. "It hurts. Why the cuffs? Am I under arrest?"

"Got a report you were involved in a shooting at a residence in Arbor Hill." He pulled my hands behind my back and cuffed me.

Did Ray report me? Why? And how would he know where I was now? "What report? Why aren't you in your patrol car? Does Curran know you're picking me up?" I looked desperately to the gym, expecting Mira to come out guns blazing any minute, or at the very least, badge flashing. She didn't.

"Got it!" Lyons called triumphantly and held up the device. "Let's get the hell outta here."

"Dunno. We were riding around off duty and an anonymous tip came in. Lyons got a scanner in the van. Worth and Davies picked up the call but he waved them off. Said we'd take it. I told him beers were on him tonight then." He slid open the Caravan door and guided me in, buckling me into the chair behind the passenger's seat.

"What tip?" I shifted uncomfortably. Seat belts were not my friend right now.

"It was a chick, dispatch said. Eyewitness with eyes on you. That's all I know." He slammed the door.

My jaw dropped along with my heart. No. No. No. No. No. That back-stabbing bitch!

Lyons got back behind the wheel, dropping the device in the center console and tossing the black backpack at Neal's feet. I got one last look at the empty doorway to the gym as we pulled out of the parking lot.

CHAPTER SEVENTEEN

I was absolutely enraged and beginning to believe spontaneous combustion could be a very real thing. Blood boiling mad was no longer a figure of speech. Who fucked who over, Special Fucking Agent? Fuck you! And fuck these two assholes.

Lyons and Neal chatted casually in front of me while Lyons blew right by the onramp to 787 that would take us back downtown. Where the police station was. He continued south on 9W.

"Where are you going?" I asked, more mad than worried.

Neal stopped talking and looked around. "Yeah, man. Where *are* you going?"

Now I was worried. Lyons is the mole and Neal isn't in on the play. I was certain. I shifted in my seat, working my cuffed hands around to my right side. "Lyons, you are a fucking stain on the badge," I said bitterly.

His gaze met mine in the rearview and his eyes crinkled with a smile I couldn't see. "The only stain is gonna be you all over the road, Sorin."

Neal glanced at me and back to Lyons. "What the hell does that mean? What's going on? Aren't we taking her in?"

We were getting away from the city, the road winding through small farm countryside between houses farther apart. I dug the knife, tacky with my blood, out from its hiding place and settled back into the seat to concentrate. I'd only successfully shimmed handcuffs open once before with my hands in front of me. My failed attempts resulted in my ratcheting them so tight I thought I was going to lose my hands. I pulled the tiny tweezers from the end of the knife, snapped it in half and got to work.

"No, Neal, we're not taking her in. I'm busting her for murder and chasing her down when she resists arrest. And when she turns on me with a raised weapon, I'm returning fire and putting two in her chest, center mass."

"What?" Neal's mouth gaped. "What the hell are you talking about? Whose murder?"

"Yours." Lyons's right hand never left the wheel and he fired across his body with his left. Neal's head snapped back, blood and brains splattering the passenger door and windshield.

"No!" I jumped, my hands jerking and the shim slipping and driving the bracelet impossibly tight around my wrist. "What the fuck, Lyons! Jesus Christ, he's your partner!"

"*Was* my partner." He met my eyes again in the mirror. Cold as ice. "By the way, that was your gun."

Be cool. Be cool. I switched the small band of metal into my left hand to try and shim the right cuff. I likely only had minutes before I lost all feeling in my hand. You got this, Sorin. You're not going out like this.

The unmistakable roar of a Harley grew louder behind us. I turned around but could only see a single bright headlight right on our ass. In the mirror, Lyons's face scrunched up in confusion, his gaze flicking from the rearview to sideview mirrors.

"Friend of yours?" I asked. He ignored me.

The Harley pulled out into the oncoming lane right alongside us. I could barely see the dimly lit rider in full helmet, visor down, long hair whipping across her back. Shade. With her left hand she made the Rat Lord's sign across her body, pointing it at Lyons before accelerating ahead of us and getting in front.

Lyons was muttering to himself, his hands opening and closing around the wheel nervously.

"Not expecting company?" I asked.

"Shut up."

"You know you're just a means to an end, right? Not really part of the club?" I lined up the shim between the single strand teeth and the lock housing. I clenched my jaw and squeezed slowly, holding my breath. The cuff tightened and the shim slid home, separating the teeth. I twisted my wrist slowly and the cuff popped open. I exhaled.

I couldn't do anything about the left cuff. It was already too tight. I left my hands behind my back and peered through the windshield in time to see Shade slow and motion to a small dark building with a large gravel turnaround up ahead. She pulled in and Lyons slowed to follow.

"Don't do it, Lyons. Means to an end makes you a *loose* end." I maybe had a chance getting past Lyons, but I wouldn't bet on getting past Lyons *and* Shade.

"Shut the fuck up, Sorin." He pulled in and around the back of what looked like a farm stand where Shade had disappeared.

The minivan's headlights lit her up. She was leaning casually against her bike—a black Fat Boy—with her arms crossed and helmet still on. Something was wrong. Or was it finally right?

Lyons got out and slid the door open, unbuckling my seat belt and ungraciously dragging me out of the van. I couldn't feel my left hand. I gripped the loose cuff in my right to keep up appearances while he marched me into the van's headlights and threw me down on my knees. Ow, goddamn it!

"Good thinking," he said. "We can set the scene, right here. I'll get her gun."

The woman straightened off the bike. I knew those clothes. I knew that body. It was the one that made my heart race, not my skin crawl.

"I'll take it from here. Griffin wants her alive."

Lyons blinked stupidly at her. "I just blew my partner's brains out in my ex-wife's minivan. How the fuck am I supposed to explain that?"

"Not my problem." She stepped closer.

"That wasn't the plan."

"Plan's changed."

He stiffened, his hand going to his sidearm. "Take off your helmet."

My heart thundered. I couldn't see her eyes until the helmet tilted down at me. I tensed, sucking in a breath, and punched up with a hard right to his balls, doubling him over with a whoosh of air and gurgle of pain. I pulled myself up on his hunched-over back and drove my right knee into his face, sending him flying into the dirt, unmoving.

I dropped back down next to him, jerking his weapon from the holster and flinging it into the field behind me. I patted his pockets for the cuff keys and jammed it into the lock as Mira, helmet off, ran over.

"Someone has been paying attention and it shows." She knelt down next to me.

I grunted, fumbling with the cuff.

"Are you all right? You knew it was me?"

"Not at first." I couldn't unlock it.

"I got it." She twisted the key and pulled the cuff with her other hand, finally popping it loose.

"Aw, shit." I rubbed my wrist and shook my hand out. "I've never wanted to gouge someone's eyes out with my thumbs before until I thought you threw me to the wolves."

"I did." She pulled me to my feet. "But I had a plan. Get your stuff. We gotta go."

I gaped at her.

"Come on, Lucky. We can fight about it later."

I ran back to the van and grabbed the backpack, making every effort not to look at Brian Neal's body. I had no love for him, but he didn't deserve this. No one did. My gun was in the console. I left it. Lyons prints were all over it. I jammed the hard drive into the backpack and met Mira at the bike. She dug in the duffel bag for the phone and thrust it at me.

I stared at it stupidly. "Who am I calling?"

"911. Officer down."

"Right." I made the call giving away nothing but the location. When they went back to listen to it they'd know it was me, but we'd be long gone.

Mira gave me a nod of approval and handed me the helmet. "I could barely see in this thing."

I jammed it on and swung my leg over the back of the bike, wrapping my arms around her waist. I never saw myself riding bitch for anyone, but I could get used to this. "I don't need to ask where you got this one."

She fired it up. "Where to?"

"Keep heading south. I know a place."

CHAPTER EIGHTEEN

An hour on the back of the bike and my head was bobbing against Mira's back. Every time my hands went slack around her waist she reached back and jabbed me in the left side to wake me up, so I wouldn't just slip off onto the road. We were outside New Paltz now, deep in the middle of land adjacent to the Mohonk Preserve, heading to my old childhood camp. It was private land at one time, then gifted to Children's Services for their use. I had no idea who owned it now. There were once official gated entrances, but they had long since fallen into disrepair and were so overgrown you wouldn't even know there was once an entrance there if you weren't looking for it.

We wound our way through the densely wooded and hilly terrain on overgrown carriage roads. Mira had to stop frequently and rattle me alert asking for directions. She had to muscle the bike around more than once and backtrack to an area that was better marked.

"Here," I mumbled through the helmet. She didn't hear me and I gave her shoulder a shake. "Stop. Stop here."

She rolled to a stop and kicked the stand down. The headlight illuminated the end of what was barely a trail. It looked like it just dropped off into nothing. She helped me off the back.

"All right?"

"Yeah." I pulled off the helmet and shook out my sweat-soaked hair. I was hot, exhausted, and thirsty. I gestured to the end of the trail. "We need to walk from here. It's too steep for the bike."

"I'll get the stuff." She collected the gray duffel and black backpack and met me at the top of the hill. "That's steep. Can't even really see the bottom."

"It's not that far, really, maybe twenty yards."

"How do you know about this place?"

"It's an old camp I used to attend as a kid. It's abandoned now. I think. I was out here a few years ago. The main building is still intact."

"How did you get down to it when you were kids?"

"Four-wheelers. It was one of the highlights of the week."

She assessed me critically. "You gonna make it?"

I shrugged. "Gonna have to. Wish I'd thought to get a flashlight, though."

"There's enough moonlight to manage. Just go slow."

"Run. Go slow. Run. Go slow. Story of my life these days," I muttered and started down, my feet immediately skidding down the hill in a barely controlled slide.

We made it to the bottom without either one of us going completely down, but there were more than a few close calls and lots of muttered curses. Not far from the base of the hill was the main house, still standing and exactly as I remembered it.

A moss-covered, white vinyl-sided, two-story house that once served as the director's quarters, dining hall and activity center. There were never more than twenty-five kids here at a time, so the space requirements weren't huge. There was a sagging wraparound porch and most of the first-floor windows were boarded up.

There used to be several smaller cabins around a central clearing that served as bunkhouses, but they had apparently been torn down. All that remained were darkened patches of packed dirt where the vegetation had yet to grow back.

"This the only building?" Mira asked, shrugging to get the bags higher up on her shoulder.

"Apparently."

"All right, then." She headed up to the house. "Let's see what we're working with."

I trudged after her and we stood together on the front porch staring at the relatively new-looking padlock secured through a very sturdy looking hasp. "Don't suppose you have a key to this one, do you?"

"'Fraid not." She arched her brow. "This is your show now, Street Crimes."

"Yep. All right. I got this one." I motioned for the backpack and Mira handed it over. I dug through it, pushing the hard drive out of the way, and triumphantly revealed the pry bar.

Her brows rose. "Aren't you clever."

"To be fair, I thought I was more likely going to bash someone's head in with this, but hey." I wedged it behind the hasp against the door.

She put a hand on my arm. "Wait."

"What?"

"That's a new lock. Someone may be using this place now. Let me just do a walk around and make sure we're alone and not walking into any ugly surprises. I've had about as much unexpected danger as I can handle for one day."

I waited anxiously for her return. It was after midnight and I was dead on my feet. I blinked and she was back *and* holding the pry bar. I looked down at my empty hands. Had I been asleep standing up?

She wedged it between the hasp and the door and with a strong jerk the hasp bent and then popped out of the wood with a ping of broken screws.

"My personal Mary Sue," I mumbled.

"What does that mean?" She headed inside.

"Is there anything you can't do?"

"Plenty of things."

"Not so far."

Mira pulled a flashlight from the duffel. She balanced it upright on the floor in the middle of the room and it was bright enough to light up most of the space.

"You couldn't have busted that out on the way down?" I asked.

"We're in hiding, remember?"

"And drove to our hideout on a Harley. Pretty sure if there's anyone around they heard us coming."

"Yeah, well, that couldn't be helped. The flashlight could," she said without turning around as she surveyed the interior.

The place may have been long ago abandoned as a camp, but someone was still using it. Hunters, maybe. The floor was relatively clean. There were two sets of bunk beds pushed against one side of the room with thin, but intact mattresses on each lower bunk.

Mira opened a battered wooden trunk to find stacks of musty but thick wool blankets.

In the middle of the vast open room, near the large fireplace filled with ash and burnt log remains, was a sturdy table with four chairs all looking sound enough. She set our gear down there. In the kitchen area, which I was all but certain wouldn't be functional as such, there were supplies across the counter—ropes, lanterns, an axe, an empty bucket and other various random tools. Stacked on the floor against the far wall beneath the one window without boards was a generous pile of wood.

The entry to the stairs leading up was boarded over and Mira gave one an experimental tug. It was solid. We weren't getting up and no one was getting down. "Is there another way in and out of here?" she asked.

"Uh..." I struggled to remember. "Yeah, uh, through the pantry in the kitchen, there's a back door."

She grabbed the flashlight, leaving me in the dark. "I'll check it out. Wait here."

I stayed put and listened to a door creaking open, scuffling, banging, thumping and then wood cracking. She came back brushing dirt and cobwebs out of her hair and off her clothes.

"I had to rip the boards off so we can get out that way if we need to. It's only ten yards to the forest from the back porch. I've jammed the door from the inside."

"Yeah, okay." I felt sick, both sweaty and cold, and struggled out of my hoodie, tossing it on the table with the rest of our meager supplies before leaning on a chair to catch my breath and my balance. "We need to call Angela."

"Not yet. Give them a minute to catch up, take care of Neal's body and question Lyons. If the people at the other end of that phone are on our side, let's give them a chance to get some answers about who all the players are."

"Why?" I wasn't following.

"We'll be safer if this gets sorted out before we go in. We don't know how high up this goes or who else may be involved."

"How long are we going to wait?" Why was all this so hard for me to understand? I was actually a good detective. I just couldn't grasp the nuances of what was going on and trying to was making me dizzy.

Mira made her way over to me. "Just long enough to get some rest. Things will be clearer in the morning and we'll be better able to handle whatever comes if we give away our position and shit goes south again."

"Sure, okay. That makes sense." I swayed on my feet.

Mira put the back of her hand to my head and grimaced. "You're pretty warm. Sit down before you fall down. We need to get that wound cleaned out and bandaged and get some fluids in you. Let's see what other miracle goodies you came away with from the house." She started rummaging through the supplies in the backpack.

"Not IV antibiotics I can assure you." I slumped into a chair.

"Wine. How romantic. None for you, I'm afraid. Or me, for that matter, but I appreciate the thought." She handed me a bottle of orange juice. "Drink all of this. Rifle through that duffel. There were some clothes I assumed were yours in the gym locker. They looked clean. Also, some toiletries."

"Cleaner than what I'm wearing anyway, which is a very low bar." I unzipped the bag and started pawing through it.

Deodorant and toothpaste. God bless. Along with clothes, my boots, and ammunition. Except I didn't even have a weapon anymore. Why the hell did I toss Lyon's service weapon? The taser she thoughtfully packed would help in a pinch, though. I pulled out my own jeans, white T-shirt and sweater along with a gloriously clean bra and underwear which I had to untangle from another… "What the hell?"

"Did you get it?" Mira asked as she set out the bandages, alcohol, and towels.

"Clearly, not. But I think I'm starting to." I held up a black external hard drive.

"What's up?" She looked up, her eyes going wide.

"Care to explain this?"

She gestured dismissively. "I picked up a blank device from the house. In case we needed to set another dummy trail."

"Really?" I stood to grab the pry bar off the table and raised it over the device. The one I had been carrying was still in the backpack. "So, you don't care if I smash it?"

"Sure, go ahead." She didn't look up, but I could see she was lying by the tense set of her shoulders. "We may still need it, though."

I swung the bar down.

"No!" She lunged for me, but I had aimed for the table, splintering off pieces of wood and clipping the side of the device leaving a gouge in the rubber casing. She pressed her lips together and sat down hard in a chair.

"I think I know who the *dummy* is in this scenario." I tossed the pry bar onto the table. "This isn't blank and it isn't from the house. I never had the real one, did I?"

"From Boomer's to the hotel, you did. I bought a new one and swapped it while you were out cold and I was picking up supplies."

"Oh, my god, I am such a fool. I actually thought when you handed me that backpack to carry because you were driving, it was because you were starting to trust me."

"Lucky, come on."

"Meanwhile, the entire time, you were concocting this plan to set me up to flush out the dirty cops. You didn't even risk the evidence, just my life." My head throbbed in time with my pounding pulse.

"There was no other way. We had to know who they were and I had eyes on you the entire time."

"Oh yeah? So, you just had keys to that dude's Harley tucked away nearby in case you needed it?"

She threw up her hands. "Okay, yeah, that took a minute. I had eyes on you *nearly* the entire time."

"That was just dumb goddamn luck the bike showed up. What were you gonna do? Rescue me in a Corolla?"

"If I had to, yeah. I would have figured something out, Lucky. I wasn't going to let them have you, I swear."

I was seriously losing it. "You could've fucking told me. What was all that bullshit about *trusting* me? Trusting *you*!"

"I couldn't tell you. It needed to be real."

A hysterical laugh bubbled up. "Oh, it was real all right. Jesus Christ, Lyons shot Neal in the head with my gun!"

"Look, Lucky, I'm sorry. I'm doing the best I can here. And you're not the only one who's lost someone to this mess. I wasn't prepared for any of this. My op was going to be finished soon. I had a ton of information. Hillis was brokering a big deal with an importer trafficking small arms through the Dark Web. He's new. Goes by the all too derivative online handle, WarDawg."

"I don't give a shit," I snarled.

She went on as if any of this meant anything to me. "In another couple of months we would've had everything we needed to get the Rat Lords *and* shut down the supplier."

"Months? What about the guns they're putting on the street *today*? What about the drugs they're putting in kids' arms *today*? What about the apartments they burned to the ground just to get at one single suspected informant that also killed innocent children?"

"I am well aware, but that's not my—"

"If you say problem, so help me god—"

"Jurisdiction. It's not *my* jurisdiction." She pointed at me, eyes blazing. "It's yours. You do *your* job and I will do *mine*."

"I was doing my job!"

"No. You were jamming up mine."

"I'm sorry, Agent Van Allen, did I interrupt your three-way at an inconvenient time?"

"Oh. Okay." She smiled bitterly. "You know, there was a lot of talk about you long before you walked through the doors of Boomer's. Your groundwork was so good you even had me convinced you'd left the badge behind. For a rookie you showed a lot of patience and ingenuity. And without backup. You played it real smart and set up a tight cover and I know plenty of what you did to make that happen."

I wasn't certain where she was going with this, but it didn't really sound like a compliment.

"Did you enjoy it? The poor bastards you hustled out of their paychecks every Friday night at the table? Women off the street looking for a quick buck that you took to the restroom just to prove you were no longer on the job, Little Miss I-Don't-Pay-For-Sex? Are you proud of yourself? You wanna call all your buds and tell them all about your latest assignment and how low you've had to sink to get the job done? You think this is fun for me? That I liked dressing like that? That I enjoyed letting a bunch of criminal assholes paw at me with their filthy hands and stinking breath?"

Her words were like a punch in the gut and I sat down hard, the anger draining out of me again and my face now flaming with regret and fever. I stared at my trembling hands for a long time. "I fucking hated it. After Sky died, I was so angry. When Angela, sort of, suggested this, I thought yes, this is what I can do for her. This is what I can do to atone. To make up for failing her when she was alive. I can get justice for her. For the ones that died in that fire. And there was no low I wouldn't stoop to to make that happen."

"You were punishing yourself," she said gently.

"Maybe." I dropped my head in my hands. "For the record, I never had sex with any of those women. I just paid them for some awkward conversation and sent them on their way after twenty minutes.

"For the record..." she replied, waiting for me to look up, "the only one of them I was physical with was Griffin Hillis. As distasteful as it was, he is at least oddly fastidious when it comes to hygiene and protection."

"What about Freezone and Ghost? I saw them going into the back with you."

She rolled her eyes. "Oh, them. They're gay for each other. They pay me quite well to be their beard."

"Really?"

"Would I lie to you?"

"Repeatedly."

"That's fair. And I'm sorry. It comes with the territory of being under for so long." She put a hand over her heart. "I'm done with that, Lucky. My cards are all on the table."

I wanted to trust her so badly. "No more secrets, Mira. No more lies."

She held my gaze. "No more secrets. No more lies."

I tried to return her smile but lurched forward and vomited at her feet instead.

CHAPTER NINETEEN

She smoothed more duct tape around my waist after spending what felt like an eternity in hell opening the wound, filling it with alcohol, stitching it up and then covering it with every clean piece of gauze she could find. "All done."

I grunted through my teeth and panted, "Sure you…passed that…medic training?"

She didn't laugh but pulled the blankets back over me and lay a cool hand across my brow. "You're shivering."

"I'm sweating balls." I was completely naked beneath a pile of wool blankets with one for a pillow.

"You're sick, Lucky, and I'm afraid it's only going to get worse until we can get you to a hospital."

She looked worried and I didn't like seeing the frown of concern on her face, especially since I was the one putting it there. I mustered a smile for her. "For someone who's not interested, you sure have a tendency to take my clothes off a lot."

That got a smile out of her. "Yeah, well, it's hard to keep a low profile when your clothes are blood-soaked." She folded another blanket and tucked it under my knees to elevate my legs a bit. "And who says I'm not interested?"

I rolled my eyes. "Thought you said no more lies."

"No lies detected."

"Oh, yeah?"

Her smile was genuine, her eyes shining. "Rain check if we live through this."

"Oh, I'm gonna live." I fell asleep to the sultry sound of her laughter.

Getting my eyes open was a struggle. My lids were heavy and grainy. While I worked on blinking the world into focus, I strained to hear anything, but it was all quiet and dark, but for the beams of moonlight cast through the one available window.

I levered myself up to my elbows and winced at the sharp pain in my side at the movement. I stilled for a minute, making sure I hadn't done any further damage. The pain receded quickly to a dull ache. Mira had done an industrial-strength job of patching me up this time. Mira.

The room was empty and my anger flared again at the thought she had left me here until I heard movement and a soft swish of fabric. I followed the sound to see the top of her head. She was in the other bunk, curled on her side and covered with a blanket. That was good, she needed sleep.

I relaxed back against the bed, my eyes drifting closed. Her shuddering breath and soft sob roused me again. Oh, god, she was crying. The sounds of her private grief filled the room and gripped my heart in a vise. My own tears streamed unchecked as all I could do was quietly share, and bear silent witness to her pain.

"Rise and shine, Street Crimes."

I blinked rapidly in the gloomy daylight of our abandoned hideaway. "I'm awake," I grumbled.

"I made breakfast."

I rolled my head to find her sitting at the table loading a spare clip for her sidearm. She was all business, save for red-rimmed eyes. Otherwise she showed no evidence of the emotion from last night that eventually led to her falling into what I can only imagine was a deep, exhausted sleep. The same kind that claimed me again not long after she fell quiet.

I remembered my nakedness in time to gather the blanket around me before swinging out of bed. Not that I had anything she hadn't already seen. Twice.

"You need to drink and eat something," she said and pushed a bottle of water and a stack of granola bars in my direction.

"I need to pee." I stood slowly. I was really sore but otherwise felt okay as long as I moved carefully. The bandages were tight and I was literally held together by duct tape now. Sleep had helped considerably. My fever felt less immediately concerning and the aches and pains from the last few days were manageable.

"There's a DIY outhouse around the side. It's been well-used, so not awesome, but better than nothing." She waved a crumpled package of wet wipes.

"Oh, yes."

"Mmm-hmm," she agreed. "It's the little things."

I snatched up the wipes and headed out. It wasn't the shower I desperately needed, but being clean-ish and in clean clothes would be a game changer.

The ground was cool and damp against my bare feet as I made my way around the side of the building to find the facilities. DIY? Nailed it. Out*house*? Not so much. Yurt, at its construction, perhaps.

I pulled aside the tattered canvas supported by several long steepled branches to find a battered mobility commode jammed into the dirt at an angle, with an open-at-both-ends five-gallon bucket beneath funneling the way into a hole in the ground, which was, unfortunately, not deep enough to avoid being able to see the mostly decomposed contents. Ugh. Alas, it served its purpose and wasn't even as bad as some of the restrooms I'd seen in the last few months. I didn't linger any longer than necessary and stepped out to make liberal use of the wipes.

Mira, the black hoodie over the clothes she was in yesterday, was rearranging the supplies in the backpack when I hustled back in, anxious to avail myself of the deodorant, suck on some toothpaste, and get dressed.

"I put a shirt out for you."

I eyed the thick black short-sleeve top on the bunk. "Got one, thanks."

"Is Hanes rated to stop rounds from a .357 Magnum?"

"Uh…" I picked up the black top. It was heavy, but thinner than I ever would have guessed body armor could be. The fabric felt just like any high-end wicking workout shirt and the flexible armored panels covered the torso front and back and wrapped around both flanks. "Oh, wow. You Feds get all the slick toys. Are you wearing one?"

"Don't worry about me."

"Mira."

"Just put it on. We have work to do."

I could tell she wasn't looking this time when I dropped the blanket and pulled on my clothes. Maybe because there were no surprises left. Maybe because we had voiced our mutual attraction and watching now would be a violation. Or maybe because given a spare second to process all that had happened, she came to the overwhelming realization I was a total loose cannon fuck-up that had caused this mess.

Stop it. This was not on me. I pushed the self-recriminations from my mind, and like her, focused on what we had to do to live to see another day.

I carefully picked at the pockets of my filthy sweats to find Sky's necklace, taking a moment to untangle the knots in the chain before replacing it safely in my pants pocket.

"Feel better?" she asked.

"Good enough for government work. What's our play? Are we leaving?" I asked as I pulled my sweater carefully over the armored shirt, smoothing everything down over the thick bandages at my waist. I tested my range of motion with a few stretches and twists to ensure my body would work in the ways I needed it to, when I needed it to. I took a chair across from her and started on the granola bars and water.

She gestured to the meager food. "Sorry. I ate the pasta salad last night."

I shrugged, happy to just be putting something in my empty stomach. "Was it good?"

"Always. Darcy puts bacon in it," she said while settling both hard drives into the backpack and zipping it closed.

I swallowed hard, the food turning to sand in my mouth and my throat closing. "Mira, I'm so sorry about your partner. I never meant for this to happen."

"I know." She offered me a tight-lipped smile.

"But you blame me."

She didn't answer for a long time and looked away, her expression unreadable. "No, I don't. You do the job, just like the rest of us. Darcy knew the risks. We all do." She finally turned back to me, her expression intense. "I don't hold what happened against you, Lucky, and you shouldn't either."

I exhaled slowly, tears threatening again. God, I was a mess. "My presence was a risk to you. How could this even happen? Why didn't we know ATF had someone under with the Rat Lords?" Someone somewhere majorly dropped a ball. Or ten.

Her eyes narrowed. "That is an excellent question. It's time to make a phone call. Things are going to move fast after that and I want to be prepared to move fast with them."

"*Things* being our execution or our extraction?"

"Hope for the best, prepare for the worst, as they say." She slid the phone across the table to me. "Whenever you're ready."

I powered on the phone to seventeen text messages from Angela and still counting as the phone immediately pinged an alert. "It's Angela."

"Your captain?"

"Hm, yeah." I snorted a laugh. "This one says she's going to keep calling until I answer or they find my body."

"Glad you can still find the humor," she said dryly and gestured to the phone. "Put it on speaker. I have questions."

The phone rang three times before there were a series of clicks and then quiet for a few long beats. "Ang? It's me."

The sharp intake of breath was audible. "Lucy, thank god. Are you okay?"

My chest clenched at the sound of her voice. It had been months since we'd talked, laughed, sparred, or argued and I ignored the invariably wise advice she offered. God, I missed her. I didn't even know how much until this moment. The likelihood I may never see her again had gone way up in the last few days and I was feeling the loss of our connection fiercely.

"Lucy, talk to me? Are you all right?" she said more forcefully.

Mira's hand reached across the table to cover mine, squeezing gently. She was here and I wasn't alone. I cleared my throat. "Yeah, um, I'm okay, Captain. We both are."

"Is Agent Van Allen with you?"

"I'm here, Captain Curran," Mira said. "Detective Sorin is not as okay as she claims. She has a lower abdomen, small arms graze that I haven't been able to treat properly in the field. We've controlled the bleeding, but she's showing signs of infection. She needs medical attention."

"She'll get it. Lucy, where are you? We'll send a team to—"

"No, Ang, I can't. It's not safe. Not until we know what's going on." I glanced at Mira and caught her nod of approval. "Did you find Lyons and…" I couldn't finish the sentence.

"We did. Officer Neal"—she cleared her throat—"Neal's body was recovered last night and Officer Lyons is in custody. We've recovered the weapon used. It's yours, which I'm sure you're aware, however you're not a suspect in Neal's death. You need to know that. Lyons has retained counsel and we haven't gotten anything out of him. Internal Affairs is handling the investigation. They'll of course be needing to speak with you, too. Both of you."

"Understood." I raked my hand through my hair.

"And the ATF safe house has been cleared?" Mira asked.

"Yes, Agent Van Allen. I'm very sorry about the loss of Agent Minor. And I expect to be able to offer my condolences in person before the end of the day."

Mira's expression tightened and she cleared her throat. "Thank you, Captain. There was a Rat Lords member there."

"We have him, too," Angela said. "He's also not being cooperative as of yet. Forbes and Monroe are taking a crack at him."

I scrubbed my hands over my face, holding back a howl of frustration. So, we still knew dick. Nothing had changed. "If

Lyons isn't talking then you don't know if anyone else on the team or in the department is working for the Rat Lords. How are we supposed to tell you where we are?"

"You know *I'm* not working for the Rat Lords, Lucy. I will get you help. No action will go through this department. I have been working closely with Special Agent in Charge Dennison. I will contact him directly and get ATF to send a team to you. They are as anxious to have both you and Agent Van Allen safe as I am. They are ready and standing by to deploy as soon as we have your location. You have to tell me where you are," she pleaded.

"Captain Curran," Mira cut in. "It was my understanding when our federal operation began last year it was with the full cooperation of Albany PD. This conflict with our UC operatives should never have happened and has severely endangered our case and our lives."

Angela sighed heavily. "You're not wrong, Agent Van Allen, and I can assure you the investigation into the incident will be comprehensive until we discover where the breakdown occurred. All I can tell you is, within the last year, our Chief of Police has changed along with much of the administrative staff. There was obviously an oversight along the way."

"Oversight?" I blurted. "Are you serious? Do you have any idea what we've been through the last few days?"

"Lucy, now is not the time for this. Those responsible will be held accountable. You have to tell me where you are. Now."

She was right. I knew it. It was time to come in. I was exhausted and scared and ready for someone else to be in charge. Mira's expression said she felt the same and she nodded. "We're at the camp where you used to visit." I didn't think anyone was listening, but just in case, only Angela would know immediately where I meant.

"Sit tight. I'll have a team there in two hours."

"We'll be here." I ended the call but left the phone on. "What now?"

Mira sat back in her chair. "Now we wait."

CHAPTER TWENTY

Time crawled as we waited. Mira insisted I sit on my ass and rest up while she kept eyes out, moving back and forth from our one available window and the door. With nothing to take my mind off it, I was too aware of my wound. It burned maddeningly and I tugged at the bandages, trying to relieve the sensation.

"We have time for me to take a look at that. See if I can make you more comfortable," she offered.

Apparently, she was keeping eyes on me, as well. "I'm all right."

She detoured from her path toward me. "You're flushed and your breathing's rapid." She snatched at my wrist before I could pull away. "Heart rate is elevated."

"Yeah, well, those are all symptoms of being scared as hell." I pulled my hand from her grasp. I felt like shit—weak, nauseated, and chilled—but there was no time to worry about it. "Which I am."

"You're not alone," she said softly and moved back to the window.

I talked just to take the edge off my nerves. "I came out here once a few years ago on the advice of my therapist. For closure, she said, and to make peace with my past."

"How'd that go?"

"This isn't the part of my past I need to make peace with, you know? But I sure as hell wasn't going to go back to those places. My memories of this place are the good ones. I got to be a kid for what felt like the first time—laughing and playing and talking stupid shit with the friends I made. I felt safe here. I learned to trust again here."

She turned. "I hope you don't lose those feelings about your time here with what's going on now."

"Mm." I hoped so, too. "What about you?"

"What about me?" She moved back to the door, cracking it open and peering out for a moment.

"You know a lot about me, but I know nothing about you except the year you graduated from the academy. How did you become a Fed?"

She closed the door and leaned her back against it. "I lost a bet."

"That was not what I expected you to say."

She smiled wryly. "Well, I do have two parents and two older brothers, however none of them are in law enforcement, if that's what you were thinking."

I really did enjoy how much she could surprise me. "Of course, being legacy law enforcement would be far too cliché for you. So, what was the bet?"

"I did my undergrad at Marist and double majored in Criminal Justice and History with every intention of going into criminal law. My best friend and I were very competitive academically, at times alternating being first in our classes. She had her heart set on the FBI. Too many *X-Files* reruns, I think."

"Mm, Dana Scully."

"Exactly. She bet me she'd do better on our final in Organized Crime, oddly enough, and if she did, I had to at least apply to the academy of my choice."

"And you took the bet even though it wasn't what you wanted?"

She shrugged. "I really didn't think I was going to lose."

"I see you've never suffered from a lack of confidence. But you did lose."

"By two points. I got a ninety-three to her ninety-five."

I winced theatrically. "Brutal. I can't believe I'm on the run with someone who only got a ninety-three in Organized Crime."

Her brows rose at the dig. "I suppose you did better?"

I smirked. "I did, but I don't want to embarrass you with the number."

She fought a smile. Perhaps she found me as delightful as I thought her? I cleared my throat. "And you went through with the bet?"

"I am a woman of my word. She, incidentally, didn't think I was going to lose either and wasn't really going to enforce the win, but the more I looked into it, the more it seemed like ATF might be a good fit for me. So..." She gestured broadly.

My gaze swept across our rustic hideaway, my mind flashing past everything that had happened in the last, I didn't even know how many days anymore. "And look at you now, running for your life from snaggle-toothed maniacs. You done good, kid."

She winked. "That's why we make the big bucks."

"Speak for yourself. And your friend? Did she make the FBI?"

"Criminal Investigative Division. She's done well. I was maid of honor at her wedding and am godmother to their two beautiful little cherubs."

"But that's not you, huh?"

"What's not?" She moved back to the window.

"Marriage?"

She was quiet a long time and didn't face me. "I came close, once. He was wonderful and supportive of my career. I'm assigned to the Albany field office but I travel a lot. I know he loved me and at the time that was enough for me to say yes to his proposal."

"But?"

She sighed heavily. "But there was just something missing for me and I couldn't name it and I couldn't explain it. It felt like I was settling, so I called it off and broke his heart."

"That must have been tough." I was definitely not sad that Mira Van Allen was not married, but I could appreciate how painful that must have been.

"It was. Causing pain to someone you love in order to put yourself and your needs first is an awful feeling. No matter how right the decision may be."

"Was it the right decision?"

"Eventually, it was for him, I think. He's married, now. We've kept in touch a little and from what I know, they're very happy."

"Was it the right decision for you?"

She turned from the window and eyed me, her gaze unwavering. "Yes. Without a doubt."

"Well, I hope you find whatever, or whomever, it is you're looking for." I said, holding her gaze.

"Uh-huh." Her mouth quirked, her eyes flashed with heat. "I'll bet."

The silence grew charged between us for several long moments until Mira adjusted her holster at her back and crossed back to the door. "I'm going up to the road."

I stood, grateful for the break in tension, or at least a change in tension. Now we can get back to the world where our lives were still on the line and stop wondering if we fit together. For the moment, the possibility of dying in a gunfight was easier for me to navigate emotionally than continuing to wonder and hope that she wanted to take a chance on me. "Good idea. We'll be able to see what's coming."

"I'm going alone."

"What? No. I need to—"

"Keep that safe." She gestured to the backpack. "It's all that matters now. This can't all be for nothing, Lucky."

I stared at it. It wasn't just every scrap of evidence against the Rat Lords and their arms supplier. It was the last year of Mira's life. Everything she'd sacrificed to get this information. It was Agent Minor's sacrifice. A federal agent tortured and murdered in the line of duty. It was Neal's sacrifice. A twenty-five-year-old beat cop shot in the head off-duty by his own partner. It was justice for Skyler. She was trusting it to me. "Why don't we just hide it somewhere?"

"And if we both get killed?"

"Right. Okay. That's terrifying and possible." I closed my eyes for a minute and inhaled deeply before slipping the backpack on and snugging the straps over my shoulders.

She handed me the taser. "I wish I had a weapon for you, but this is the best I can do."

I adjusted it in my grip. "I'll manage."

"I'm only going as far as the top of the hill. I'll be able to hear and see anyone coming to the end of the road. If anything looks off, I'll get back down here and we're out, so be ready for me."

I grinned crookedly. Shoot your shot, Sorin. Do it. Don't wait. You could be dead in an hour. "I'll be ready for you."

She shook her head, but couldn't hide her smile. "Lucky, if this goes bad—"

My hand on her cheek stopped her words. My lips against hers, stopped my heart. There was no hesitation from either of us. No sensual teasing or promises to come. Just raw, bruising passion built from shared desire, and fear we may never get another chance.

She crushed her lips to mine with a low groan, her body pressed hard against me, her hands raking across the back of my neck to pull me in close. The weight of her body against mine kindled a fire in me not from fever alone and the world melted away. For a moment there was only us and we were safe.

I pulled away first, both of us breathing heavily, her eyes bright with the longing I shared. "Rain check," I whispered.

She cupped my cheek, her smile bittersweet. "Rain check." And then she was out the door.

I paced and imagined I could hear the second hand of my watch ticking away long minutes. I checked the taser. I looked out the one window into nothing. I tightened the backpack. I listened at the door for any sign of movement. I took a swallow of water. And choked when I heard the crunch of footsteps outside, slow across the ground then the thump of a boot on the deck. I backed away from the door and raised my weapon.

The door opened slowly and two hands emerged, fingers splayed. "Lucky? Please, tell me you're in there. It's me. If you're armed, don't shoot."

My heart hammered in my chest. Ray's head popped out from behind the door as he stepped in slowly. "Don't tase me, bro."

"What the fuck, Ray?" I gasped. "Where's Mira?"

"Who?" He frowned and stepped in all the way, making sure I could see his hands.

"Agent Van Allen. Where the hell is she?"

He stepped closer. "I have no idea. I didn't see anyone else."

I backed up, my finger tightening on the trigger. "Stay where you are! How did you find me?"

"I went back to your apartment. Still trashed by the way. I found the photo of you and Curran at a camp when you were a kid and looked it up. I just took a chance when I realized that it would be a straight shot from where the shit with Lyons and Neal went down. I'm so fucking glad I found you."

I eyed him, my gaze flicking to the unboarded window on my left. Where the hell was Mira? "Are you alone? Why are you here, Ray?"

"Yeah, I'm alone. Curran had me riding a damn desk until we brought you in. Didn't want my emotions getting in the way. Funny coming from her. And why do you *think* I'm here? I've been going out of my goddamn mind worrying about you." He reached in his pocket. "Look—"

"Don't!" This can't be happening. This was Ray. Ray would never hurt me. Right? His sidearm was holstered at his hip. Right?

"Easy. Easy." He held up one hand and pulled the other slowly from his pocket. "It's just this." He unfolded a five-dollar bill and showed it to me.

I frowned at it and stepped closer. "Put it on the table."

He set the bill on the table and stepped back, keeping his hands raised. "Look familiar?" From the corner of my eye I watched him while I studied the bill. It was Spocked and looked exactly like the one I had shown Ray the night of the raid on Chumps. The night I was arrested and held for three days. My cash had never been returned to me.

"How did you get this?"

"I saw it in the coffee collection can this morning."

"That doesn't tell me anything. Anyone in processing could have taken it."

"Sure, yeah, but why would someone from processing be putting up money for coffee for Street Crimes?"

He had a point and I rolled that around in my head. "So, Lyons got a hold of it and donated coffee money with my cash?"

Ray shook his head. "It wasn't there yesterday. The can was empty except for a few loose coins. It showed up sometime this morning."

I sucked in a breath. Not Lyons. He'd been in custody since last night. Someone else was involved with the Rat Lords. Someone who had access to my stuff in holding. Someone who likely made sure Griffin Hillis ended up with my cue to get me out to the club and get a read on me and what I'd been up to since I left the force.

I released a slow breath and lowered my weapon with shaky arms. "Any idea who?"

"Yeah, and it's fucked—"

The one window exploded in a spray of glass and Ray spun and went down. A split second later I heard the shot. Instincts took over and I flipped the table and dropped into a crouch behind it, putting it between me and the window. I stared at Ray a few feet away—unmoving and blood covering his face. "Ray? Ray!"

Fuck. Fuck. Fuck.

There was noise outside the door before Mira burst in and dove across the floor, weapon drawn, landing next to me. "Why did you do that?" I screamed. "Mira, what the hell?"

"Shh, shh, shh. Lucky, I didn't fire. It's not me. We're in trouble." She looked me over. "Are you hurt?"

"What…no, I'm…who…" So many things I wanted to say and I couldn't form a single thought.

"Out the back. Stay down." She pushed me toward the kitchen.

I resisted. "What about Ray?"

She pinned me with a look as serious as I'd even seen her. "We can't help him if we're dead. Now move."

"Who's firing?" I panted as we duckwalked out from behind the relative safety of the table. My side burned with the motion and I felt the all too familiar pop and sting of busted stitches.

"I don't know. If Curran was to be believed it's too soon for my team and they wouldn't be trying to kill me."

"Oh yeah? What's that like?"

"Sorry. My guess is the shooters are either Rat Lords or someone working for them."

I froze, my heart dropping. "Ray led them here?"

She pushed on my back to get me moving again. "I don't think so. At least, not intentionally. I saw Keller come in driving an unmarked. He drove all the way to the end of the road. He was alone. He wandered around the top of the hill, found the bike I stashed and headed down. Never drew his weapon, never made a call or gave a signal. I trusted you could handle him, so I stayed where I was out of sight just to be sure."

We'd made it safely into the pantry without further incident. I stood and gripped my side. "Fuck," I hissed. "And then?"

She pushed past me, kicking the boards wedged between the door handle and the floor out of the way, and shouldered the weathered door open. It groaned on its hinges. "Come on. And then a silver Jag pulled up. Sound familiar?"

"No idea. Someone on the Rat Lords payroll, no doubt."

"They stopped too far off and I couldn't see who was in the car and I didn't stick around to find out. I couldn't stay hidden and move fast enough to beat them down to the cabin. I had to circle around through the woods."

"No bikes, though?"

I followed her out into the afternoon sun, blinking as my eyes adjusted.

"Not so far." On cue, the unmistakable rumble of Harleys could be heard not far off and getting closer.

"Welp, the gang's all here," I muttered. We stopped and

listened for a moment, hearing engines cut out one after the other. "I heard three."

"Yeah. For now." Mira checked her watch. "My team should be here soon. We just need to stay out of the line of fire until then." She stepped off the small back porch at a low run and headed for the tree line.

I was almost into the trees when I slowed, my mind whirling. "Wait. If the bikers are just getting here that means it was a cop who shot Ray?" The words were barely out of my mouth when more shots fired, one round thunking into the ground at my feet, and another splintering the tree bark near my head.

Mira jerked me off my feet the rest of the way into the brush, covering me with her body. "What did I just say, Street Crimes? Stay the hell down!" she yelled over two more shots ripping through the foliage above us. She rolled to her side, firing three rounds in the general direction of the shooter. "Move! Move!"

I ran. My legs pumped, my lungs burned, my side ached, and my heart pounded. The shooting stopped for the moment, and Mira crashed through the dense forest behind me. I had to get my head out of my ass and get my bearings. Out of however many people were running around these woods at the moment, I was the only one who was even remotely familiar with the area. That was our advantage.

I slowed and Mira plowed into me, nearly knocking me off my feet. "Wait." I grabbed her arm for balance and to stop her.

"What's wrong?"

"I need to think for a minute or we'll end up getting pinned or running in circles." I straightened and looked around. We could no longer see the back of the building. I turned in a slow circle. The playing fields would be useless. Even with years' worth of growth they were flat and wouldn't provide enough cover. Same with the archery range, which wasn't anywhere near our present location.

"Speed it up, Lucky. We can't stay here." Mira stayed crouched, weapon drawn and shifting to any rustle of undergrowth nearby.

Oh, god, think. We needed to be protected. We needed to

see. We needed to defend ourselves. High ground. "King of the hill," I blurted, finally.

Mira must be getting used to my scattered outbursts by now. She didn't even question me. "Lead the way."

CHAPTER TWENTY-ONE

We hadn't gone far when a branch cracked loudly behind us and Mira whirled, dropping to one knee, weapon raised.

"I just want to talk," a man called out.

"Hillis?" Mira's weapon darted back and forth, unable to get a location on him. It was midday and clear skies, but the forest was dense and the shadows long, providing plenty of cover.

"Come on, don't be like that, kitten. Wasn't so long ago you were calling me Daddy. That is, when your mouth wasn't full."

Mira didn't respond to his vile taunting except to narrow down his location, but my stomach turned on her behalf. She shifted position, training her weapon on a large oak to our right ten yards away. Griffin Hillis, wearing jeans and leather jacket without a shirt, stepped out from behind the tree, arms raised.

"Stay behind me and stay alert," she commanded. "He's trying to distract us."

I turned in a slow circle, taser drawn. It wasn't much, but it was something. I only had one shot and they'd need to be within twenty feet of me. And if I missed…

"I'm not armed, kitten," Hillis said.

"Bullshit," Mira snapped. "Lift up your jacket. Turn around."

I remained watching our backs. My skin prickled warnings from all sides. Mira could handle Hillis, but she didn't have eyes in the back of her head and we knew he wasn't alone. There had to be at least three of them now, maybe more. Probably more. The forest gave away nothing, considering there were several armed criminals crashing around out there. We had been in one place too long already and alarm bells screamed in my head.

"See, I told you," he said triumphantly, his footsteps getting closer.

"That's far enough," Mira warned.

"Just shoot him, Mira," I said over my shoulder.

"He's unarmed." Her bitterness and frustration were unmistakable.

"Then let me shoot him." I turned to face them, intending to tase the shit out of Griffin Hillis, when the brush nearby exploded with crashing branches and a bellow of rage. Powerful arms wrapped around me from behind, squeezing the breath from me and lifting me from my feet.

"Lucky!" Mira yelled.

I couldn't help her, but I had a front row seat when Hillis made his move, lowering his right arm until a sub-compact concealed in his sleeve dropped into his hand.

Shots popped off around me and Mira returned fire, but I had no energy to spare as I struggled to breathe and my side screamed in agony. I didn't know who had me and I didn't care. He was strong as hell and wanted to kill me. I fought for my life.

My head whipped back, cracking him in the face with a satisfying crunch, followed by my right heel kicking back hard into this shin. His hold loosened with a howl of pain. As soon as my feet hit the ground my right fist hammered into his groin. I twisted, spinning hard with a right elbow to his throat then left palm strike to his damaged nose sending him to his knees.

It was Thor. Of course. I tagged him good, but even from his knees he wasn't that much shorter than me and he was far from down and out. I raised the taser, but he knocked it out of my hand with an enormous fist. Swinging back, that same fist caught me across the jaw in a powerful backhand that staggered me. I swallowed blood.

He lurched to his feet, blood pouring from his nose and mouth and dripping off the end of his stupid wannabe Viking beard. He snarled menacingly and I was delighted to see he was down a tooth. Despite the damage, I was too slow to avoid the boot he drove into my side. I went down hard, too breathless to even cry out.

I whooped gasping breaths, my vision graying at the edges, and pushed against the ground with my feet and elbows, inching away from him as he advanced on me. My right arm struck something hard and I groped for it, getting a solid grip.

From close range the barbs stuck deep into both sides of his thick chest—shoulda worn your leather, asshole—and twelve-hundred volts with a side of three milliamps surged down the wires. He went rigid. I scrambled out of the way as he fell forward onto his damaged face like a felled tree.

"This is for Sky, you piece of shit." I pulled the trigger again to give him another five-second jolt. His body jerked and then went still.

"Nice work, Street Crimes." Mira crouched next to me and placed a hand on my shoulder. "You all right?"

"Uh…yeah, maybe. I don't know. Jesus." My heart pounded and everything hurt. Some things more than others. Way more. "Are you? Shit, your arm." Her sleeve was torn, her skin bloody beneath.

"It's just a scratch." She helped me to my feet and looked me over, wiping blood from my mouth with her thumb. "We gotta move. The others will follow the shots."

I let her propel me through the woods, too dazed to do much else. "Hillis?"

"Not going anywhere. Shot him in the legs."

"Both?" I stumbled, going down to one knee, pain flaring along my side. Mira's arm hooked around my waist and hauled me up and I couldn't stifle the cry of pain that tore through me. "We gotta get…to high ground."

Mira took some of my weight like the hero that she was. "Forget it. My team will be here in minutes. Let's just get to the road."

My head swam and vision wavered. Blood loss? Exhaustion? Infection? All of the above? I fumbled with the straps of the backpack, trying to get it off while Mira dragged me along. "Just take this and go."

Mira gripped me tighter and kept up our ragged pace, cutting back through the trees toward the camp. "I'm not leaving you."

"The evidence is the only thing that matters, remember?" My head rolled loosely on my shoulders. Up was down and down was spinning. My stomach threatened to make its contents known.

"Just shut up and stay with me. I'm not losing anyone else."

We stopped when we came to the edge of the tree line at the campgrounds again. We were either further away from the main cabin than where we started, or my vision really was messed up. We were facing one end, now. Unfortunately, the far end, making the distance to the road that much farther. But, from this angle, we could see most of the front and the back at the same time. Mira let go of me and I dropped gratefully onto the ground. Even through my clothes, the damp ground felt cool against my overheated skin. "We're in the weeds now, huh?" I tittered.

"Shh, shh, shh." Mira crouched and laid a hand on my leg while never taking her eyes off the front of the cabin. "Shade's watching the cabin."

"Oh, goody. Gonna smear that bitch all over this—"

"Not this time, Lucky." She changed the magazine in her weapon and racked the slide before pressing it into my hand.

I blinked at her stupidly until my brain caught up with what was happening. "Don't you fucking dare."

Mira forced a smile. "It will be okay."

"No, it won't. Mira, she's deranged."

"Lucky, stop." Mira cupped my cheek. "Listen to me."

I couldn't help but lean into her soothing touch. "Okay."

"Stay here until I have her attention and then follow the tree line around the back of the house and back to the road."

I frowned and shook my head. "There's still an unknown fourth. There has to be. Who drove the Jag?"

"I know." Mira nodded. "Once I engage Shade, whoever is left is bound to show themselves. Just make sure you keep out of sight until then."

"No, Mira, no." I was too exhausted and too terrified to control my emotions and couldn't stop the frustrated tears from spilling over. "They'll kill you."

Mira leaned in to gift me with the sweetest lingering kiss. When I opened my eyes to meet her gaze her eyes flashed wickedly. "They'll try."

She was gone before I could do anything but watch from the trees as she made her way out into the open and began a slow walk toward the front of the house, twenty yards away.

"I'm not armed," Mira announced. She held her hands out from her sides as she advanced toward Shade, who had dressed to menace with a shoulder holster over her black tank showing off thick, tattooed arms. She trained her weapon on Mira as soon as she saw her.

"I want the device," Shade called back and fired at Mira's feet. The round struck the dirt several yards in front of her. Mira didn't flinch but she stopped just the same.

"I don't have it."

"Bitch, get it. I'm not playin'." Shade fired again. I jumped, but Mira held her ground.

She shook her head and raised her voice. "No chance. It's on its way to the police as we speak. And the police are on their way here, so choose wisely what you do next."

Goddammit, I hear you. I'm going. I'm going. I started picking my way carefully along the tree line toward the back of the cabin. Keeping one ear on the fading conversation and both eyes on the ground in front of me.

There was no more talking that I could hear. Move, Sorin. Jesus. Don't let her down. Two more shots rang out and someone screamed. The quiet that followed had a finality to it that had my pulse racing. I picked up the pace. As much as I could anyway, with my left arm supporting me from tree to tree and my right, gun in hand, pressed against my side to keep my guts from spilling out. I'm sure that wasn't really a concern, but it sure as hell felt like it. My awkward ambling left me just one stumble away from blowing my own foot off.

I couldn't hear anything anymore and I had no idea if that was good or bad. If I couldn't hear them, hopefully they couldn't hear me. I wasn't even trying to be quiet anymore and broke into a limping jog through the forest behind the back of the house.

"Sorin! I know you're out there." A new, but all too familiar voice called out and stopped me in my tracks. "Got Agent Van Allen here. She's got something to say to you."

"Lucky, go! Get to the—" Mira cried out and though I couldn't see them with the cabin between us I was close enough to hear the unmistakable sound of her being pistol-whipped.

I used the side of the cabin now for support while I made my way around. Where the hell was Angela? How long had it been? It felt like years. Please, don't shoot me in the head. At least I was wearing clean underwear.

I paused for a beat at the side of the cabin and straightened up. I wiped blood from my face with the sleeve of my sweater, and sweat from my palms against my pants, before adjusting my grip on my gun. Mira's gun. I stepped around to the front, weapon at the ready. "I'm here."

"Sorin," Michelle Monroe greeted, her left arm snaked tightly around Mira's throat and her right held her police issue sidearm against her temple. Mira's right eye was swelling and there was blood running freely from a gash along her hairline. Her left arm hung limply and her right hand gripped the thick forearm across her throat trying to keep her airway open. Her strained breathing was still audible from twenty feet away. Shade lay unmoving several feet away.

"Monroe." I was so tired. I tried to be shocked at seeing her, but I just didn't have the energy to process one more thing. I lowered my weapon. I wasn't going to shoot her with Mira in the line of fire, and she knew it. "What do you want?"

"What the hell do you think?"

Mira tensed. "Don't give it—"

"Shut up." Monroe tightened her hold, cutting off her words with a strangled grunt. "Lose the gun, Sorin. Give me the device."

"I have it." I tossed my weapon into the dirt. Far enough away to show my compliance, but still close enough to me that with an amazing feat of athleticism, I could get to it again. What the hell, Angela? Where are you? I hooked a thumb over my shoulder. "It's in the backpack."

Monroe took a step toward me, forcing Mira along. "Get it. Hurry up."

I dragged the backpack from my shoulders and dropped it at my feet, crouching down and ripping the zipper open.

"Slowly," Monroe yelled.

I barked a laugh. "Which is it, Monroe? Jesus."

She snarled, "I want to put a bullet through your fucking skull so bad."

"Yeah, well, you're not the first." I groped around in the backpack until my hand landed on the external drive—the one with the undamaged case.

"Throw it over."

"Lucky, don't," Mira wheezed, struggling against Monroe's hold.

I held Mira's gaze as I stood. "I'm not losing anyone else, either." I tossed the hard drive toward Monroe. It hit the ground and bounced and all the things happened at once.

Monroe moved her weapon from Mira's head and aimed for the device, Mira drove her elbow into Monroe's gut and spun out of her hold, and I dove to the right for the gun, fumbling it into my hands. I got my hands on it, but not before Monroe put two rounds into the hard drive and two into Mira's chest, blowing her backward.

"Mira!" I raised my weapon to Monroe.

"Put it down, Sorin," a deep voice boomed.

I rolled my head to see Forbes, gun drawn moving toward us. I groaned, letting the Sig fall from my hands, and rolled onto my back, staring up at the clear afternoon sky. I was done. I didn't care anymore. Just shoot me.

"You, too, Michelle," he commanded, training his weapon on Monroe. "I *will* shoot you."

"Federal Agents!" Men and women in black tactical gear swarmed down the hill, out from behind the cabin and from the tree line.

Oh. Okay. Don't shoot me. I struggled to my hands and knees and crawled over to Mira.

"Hey, hey. Don't move." Her eyes were wide, her lips parted and throat working around words that wouldn't come. Her right hand clawed feebly at her chest. I unzipped her hoodie expecting to see her chest in tatters. Her shirt was black and thick, with two rounds lodged in the plates covering her left breast.

She sucked in shallow ragged breaths, wincing with every inhale. Still her mouth quirked into a smile. "You think…I only had one…and gave it…to you?"

My mouth gaped and I sat back on my heels, staring at her in disbelief. "Sneaky bitch."

"Had to…be real." She tugged at the shirt. "Pull the… plates."

I felt along the seams until I could grasp the flexible panel over her chest and ease it out of the insert sleeve. The layered composite fabric was distorted from the rounds and I tossed it aside, not wanting to see how close she'd come to death. ATF would need to collect it at some point. Her breathing deepened slightly without the added weight and pressure. "Better?"

She nodded. "Thanks."

"Did you shoot Shade?"

She shook her head and winced. "Monroe is…terrible shot."

"She tagged you pretty good."

"Was point-blank." She reached for my hand, the strength of her grip letting me know how much pain she was in. "Debrief next."

I ran a grimy hand through my grimy hair while the crime scene buzzed around us, comms chattered, orders were barked and the distant thump of helicopter blades grew louder. "I was kinda hoping they'd at least do a drive-by of the nearest hospital. I'm fine, but you're a bit of a mess."

"They'll separate us."

"I know the drill." I did in theory, but this case was huge. Ray would say it's a shit sandwich and everyone was gonna get a bite. Oh, Jesus, Ray. There was a dead Fed, a dead cop—maybe two, definitely two dirty ones, and the list of crimes, suspects and charges to match them with was enormous. Mira and I were key witnesses in all of it and we would be kept from each other until the case was airtight. "Won't be forever."

"Long time."

"You say that like you're gonna miss me." I mustered a cocky smile.

"Maybe." She managed a smile. "You did it, Lucky."

"And you let the bad guys get the drop on you," I scoffed, raising her good arm to kiss the back of her knuckles.

She smiled through her obvious pain. "*Let*, being the… operative word."

I gaped at her. "You set me up again?"

"I trusted you…to save my life. And you did."

I snorted. "Well, as it turns out we were moments from being rescued, so…"

"Don't sell yourself short."

"Lucy!"

I turned at Angela's voice and all the terror and pain of the last few days, few months overwhelmed me, bringing tears again. "Hey, Ang."

She knelt on the ground and pulled me gently to her. "Thank, god, Luce. Thank you, god."

We held each other for a moment before she pulled away, worry and relief etched into her features. She turned to Mira whose breathing was alarmingly shallow. "Hang in there, Agent Van Allen, paramedics are on the way."

"Ma'am," she whispered. "Nice to finally…meet you."

Angela's voice was tight with emotion. "Thank you for keeping her safe."

Mira's gaze dragged to mine, her mouth hinting at a smile. "Other way…'round."

The moment was too much and I breathed a hysterical laugh that turned into a sob of exhaustion, and then vomited into the grass.

CHAPTER TWENTY-TWO

Who's talking so loud? Why does my mouth taste like this? Oh, god, why does my head hurt so bad? My side? My…body?

"Should you be in here?"

"You gonna order me to leave?"

"No. She'll need you now."

"She'll have me. Always."

"She's waking up."

"Lucy? Can you hear me? Can you open your eyes?"

A hand squeezed mine. Ow. I unstuck my tongue from the roof of my mouth and blinked Angela into focus. "Stop shouting."

"Hey there. You're going to be okay." She smiled at me and moved from my line of sight. "Look who's here."

Mira? I rolled my eyes toward the end of the bed. "Ray," I croaked.

He wheeled himself over to the side of the bed and reached for the hand not covered in tape and tubing. His head was wrapped in gauze and what hair I could see had been shaved to the scalp. "Hey, dude. You scared the shit outta me."

"You're the one that got shot in the head," I rasped and started coughing for my efforts.

He smirked and waved me off. "Just a flesh wound."

"And a grade-three concussion, Detective Keller. I expect you to follow doctors' orders as you would mine." Angela pressed a half-full plastic cup with a bendy straw into my hands. "And you're not allowed much to drink yet. You're on all IV fluids, antibiotics and pain meds," she explained.

I stared at her. "How long have we been here?"

"About a day," she said.

I rolled a little water around in my mouth before swallowing. "Where's here?"

"MidHudson Regional in Poughkeepsie."

"Is Mira here, too?"

Ray smirked knowingly, but Angela managed to keep it professional. "Agent Van Allen got flown to Albany Med's trauma unit. She has some broken ribs and internal injuries. She's serious but stable and expected to make a complete recovery."

A knot of fear in my chest loosened and brought with it a wave of exhaustion weighing down my eyelids and slowing my thoughts. "Good. That's good. What about—"

"Stop talking," Angela said and took the cup from me before it slipped from my fingers. "Griffin Hillis and his associates, the ones you know as Shade and Thor, are being treated under guard for serious injuries, but all are expected to be fit to stand trial when the time comes. ATF is taking over the Rat Lords' case and we're letting them. We have our own mess to clean up. Along with Lyons, Michelle Monroe is in custody. Al Forbes is on administrative leave until he's been cleared by Internal Affairs of any involvement. You'll need to be debriefed as soon as possible. The mayor and the chief are preparing a joint press conference to tout the end of the Rat Lords stranglehold—their words—on the city. They're very pleased."

"Well, as long as they're happy," Ray grumbled.

Angela shot him a look of disapproval, but there was no real heat behind it. "The chief texted me this a few hours ago. Asked that I show you." She handed me her phone.

I frowned at the message, my tired eyes unwilling to focus for a long moment. "Medal of Honor?"

"Damn, Lucky." Ray rocked back in his wheelchair and slow clapped. "Beats the hell outta my Purple Heart for gettin' shot in the melon. You'll get one of those, too, I bet."

Angela took the phone from me. "There will be a more formal announcement and ceremony later on."

"Whatever." I shrugged. I didn't care. My heart hurt. My body hurt. I was so goddamn tired.

A series of emotions crossed Angela's face, a mix of concern, pride and relief. "You're going to be okay, Lucy."

"Yeah," I whispered, my throat constricting painfully. "What about...what about WarDawg?"

"I beg your pardon?"

"The, um, arms dealer ATF was after. Their case..."

"Oh." She frowned. "He's offline. ATF Cybercrimes is following his trail, but as of yesterday he's gone dark. They can't track him."

"Fuck."

"That's not for you to worry about, Lucy. You just need to focus on healing, right now. I have this for you, too." She reached in her pocket and pulled out my gold shield.

My pride and joy. I stared at it but made no move to take it. I couldn't yet. It was different. I was different. I didn't know how yet, but I knew just the same.

Angela seemed to understand. "It will be waiting for you whenever you're ready. No pressure. No rush." She slipped the shield back into her pocket and removed something else, a gold chain with an *S* pendant, and pressed it into my shaking hand. "Hold on to this one, though, Lucy. For as long as you need."

I cried again. Why did caring have to hurt so much? "Thanks, Ang."

She nodded, her own eyes bright with emotion. "I'll let you get some rest. There's a local patrol stationed outside your room. I'll be back tomorrow to pick you both up."

"Thanks, Captain," Ray said.

I didn't try to stop the tears and I was too damn tired to wipe them away.

Ray cleared his throat. "You want me to, um…I should go and let you get—"

"Stay," I whispered and held out my hand for him. "Please."

He took my hand tightly in both of his. "I'm really fucking glad you're not dead, Lucky," he finally blurted.

I grunted a laugh. "I'm really glad you're not dead either. Or on the take."

"You didn't really think that, did you?"

"No," I breathed. "No, I didn't. Not telling you what was going on was the hardest thing about this mess."

"Bet it wasn't as hard as your lady boner for that Fed."

I barked a laugh and winced at the pain it caused. "Shit, I've missed you."

"I approve, by the way."

"Oh, do you? Good, 'cause I was just gonna ask for your permission."

"Any idea when you're going to see her again?"

"No." I tried not to think about that. She was going to recover and she was with her people and that was going to have to be enough for now. If I talked about it anymore I may never stop crying. "Listen, I was thinking maybe when we get out of here, I'll pick us up some pizza and beer and maybe you can come over and help me put my place back together. You know, if you want."

He grinned. "Make it a bucket of chicken and you got a deal."

My eyes flew open when I lurched against the seat belt and it cut into my side. "Aw, damn. What the hell?"

"Sorry. I'm sorry. Are you okay? The lady ran right in front of me," Angela said from behind the wheel of her SUV.

"She's in a wheelchair, Captain," Ray quipped.

I'd fallen asleep as soon as we'd gotten in the car, me in the back 'cause the pain meds made me drowsy and Ray in the front, so he wouldn't throw up from his brain still sloshing around inside his skull. We were a pair. "Why are we back at the hospital?"

"It's Albany Med," Angela said as she pulled over into a thirty-minute pickup and drop-off spot near the main entrance.

"Why?" She was supposed to be taking me home and a patrol car was going to be assigned to my apartment for the time being. ATF was moving fast, relatively speaking, but federal warrants took time and until all the club members who could be implicated and charged were in custody it was especially unsafe to be me.

Angela turned, her arm over the back of the passenger seat. "ATF Special Agent in Charge Dennison is expecting you. At my request."

"My idea," Ray piped up.

"He's allowing you a few minutes to visit. If you want."

I stared at her for a long moment, blinking stupidly, before the penny dropped. "With Mira? Did she ask for me?"

Angela's brow furrowed. "No. She's…no, she didn't ask. He's waiting for you in the lobby. We'll wait here."

It was only a few yards to the main entrance sliding doors, but apparently far enough for me to get winded. SAIC Dennison wasn't hard to spot. He had to be the tall slender guy in the suit with gray hair and slightly goofy ears. He was talking into his phone without moving his mouth while his gaze darted around the lobby.

He apparently already knew what I looked like and waved me over as he ended his call. "Detective Sorin. Pleased to see you up and around."

"Thank you, sir." I shook the hand he offered. "It's good to meet you."

"We met already, but I'm not surprised you don't remember. You were pretty out of it." He walked briskly toward the elevators on long legs and I struggled to keep up.

"I'm doing much better."

"Good. I'd appreciate it if you and your captain would make an appointment by the end of the week for a full debrief at my office. The sooner the better," he added, without further niceties and stabbed the button for the fourth floor with a long finger.

This guy was serious and I couldn't blame him one bit. "Yes, sir. Of course. Whatever I can do to help you get the case resolved."

He stared straight ahead at the closed elevator doors. "*Salvaged* would be the term I would use."

Damn, he was not pulling punches. I had no idea if he was naturally curt, exceptionally businesslike, extremely pissed, or something else entirely. "Yes, sir."

When the doors opened on the fourth floor, he strode out without a gesture to me, and again I pushed my body to match his pace without having to break into a jog, which was likely impossible in my current condition.

He nodded at the agent standing sentinel at the door to a private room near the nurses' station. "Detective Sorin has ten minutes. No more."

"Sir." The agent nodded and pushed the door open for me.

I was confused and couldn't help but ask, "Why are you allowing this? Isn't this against regulations?"

SAIC Dennison eyed me. "A courtesy to Captain Curran. I'm not concerned that you and Agent Van Allen are going to conspire to change your statements, if that's what you mean."

"No, sir. Of course not." Okay. He either trusted me or trusted Mira. Probably not me. I stepped into the room as the nurse finished entering vitals into the small laptop on the wheeled cart next to the bed. Or, the option I hadn't considered—Mira was on a ventilator. "What the hell?"

Her dark hair fanned against the crisp white hospital bedding and faded hospital gown, the bruising on her face a stark contrast to her unusually pale complexion. An endotracheal tube was taped in her mouth and the beep and hiss of machines sounded rhythmically, announcing every heartbeat and breath.

"I know it looks scary, dear," the older nurse said. "Pulmonary contusions can be very serious. This is only temporary until her lungs heal a bit and her oxygen saturation improves."

"Jesus." I moved closer to the bed. I could see her eyes moving beneath her lids but her arms lay still against her sides, her wrists wrapped in thick gauze and tied to the bed rails. My heart lurched. "Why is she restrained?"

"She's only sedated enough to tolerate the ET tube, which she was not happy about needing. If patients are determined and capable enough, and I'm certain Agent Van Allen is both those things, they can try to pull it out and cause further damage."

My chest squeezed and tears threatened again seeing her like this. "How long, um, will she have to be…"

"She's strong and doing really well. If that continues she should be extubated tomorrow morning and on supplemental oxygen only. Barring any unforeseen setbacks, as long as her pain is well controlled, she should be out of here by the end of the week. You're family?"

"Oh, uh, no. I'm…" What? What am I to her? A witness? A colleague? A pain in her ass? "I'm just a friend."

"Well, friend, you didn't hear any of that for me. And you must be a good one if that robot outside let you in." She squeezed my arm gently on her way out the door. "Talk to her, dear. She can hear you."

"Five minutes," the robot outside announced before the door closed on the nurse's exit.

Shit. Shoot your shot, Sorin. I held her fingers loosely, running a shaky thumb over the back of her hand. Nothing changed that I could tell that suggested she knew anyone was touching her.

"Hey, Mira, it's me." I winced. "I mean, it's Lucky. I'm probably not, you know, *me* to you, yet. Or, maybe ever. Uh, sorry, I don't even know what I'm saying. I'm nervous and on pain meds. I'm usually smoother with the ladies. What? Jesus, I hope your nurse was lying about you being able to hear me. She's lovely, by the way. Your nurse, I mean."

The door cracked open. "One minute, Detective."

"Uh, yeah, be right out," I called over my shoulder before turning my attention back to her. "Anyway, I think…I mean, I know I'm gonna be okay. Thanks to you." I gave her hand a final gentle squeeze. "You're going to be okay, too, Mira."

CHAPTER TWENTY-THREE

Hey, Google, how many days is it acceptable to keep an ATF Special Agent in Charge waiting before going in for a debrief after royally fucking his case? No days? Five days, it is. And five days took me to the ass end of the window Dennison gave me.

That's how many days of appointments with my therapist it took me to be able to look at myself in the mirror. How many days it took for the bruises to fade. The physical ones, anyway. How many days it took me to be able to change the bandage on my side and look at the ragged, healing wound that would scar dramatically following the infection I was still on antibiotics for, without shuddering from the memories of how I earned it. Five days to stop seeing Mira, the strongest, most courageous person I'd ever met, on a ventilator every time I closed my eyes. It would take many more days still to quiet the nightmares that woke me up sweating, my heart threatening to pound right out of my chest.

I dressed carefully in front of the mirror, forcing myself to confront the person I knew I was becoming. Except for the scar and a few less pounds, I looked no different. But I knew now, without a doubt, I didn't want to keep going through life feeling so disconnected from those around me—or pretending, too, anyway. Angela knew I was never as distant as I wanted to think. Now, it felt like the time to start leaning into human connection, not away from it.

Ray came over to help me put my place back together as promised. We shared chicken and beer even though neither one of us were supposed to be drinking. We laughed about stupid shit like friends do. I bought a laundry hamper and some shelves for stuff. Ray bought me an alabaster statue of a nude woman to put on it. I was going to buy more than just two sets of sheets and towels, more than just one set of dishes and maybe some glasses, so if anyone actually accepted an invitation to come over I could serve them a drink. I bought groceries.

I took a deep breath in and exhaled slowly before straightening the collar of my long-sleeve, black button-down beneath the charcoal plaid jacket I bought for the occasion. Look good, feel good, right?

"Detective Sorin. Right on time," Angela greeted me in the lobby of the ATF field office. She looked me over, her expression approving. She'd stopped by my place a few times since I got released from the hospital, but this was the first time we'd seen each other in a professional capacity. "You're looking well."

"Thank you, Captain. Ready?"

"Are you?"

I shrugged and offered her a wry smile. "As I'll ever be."

Her mouth quirked up. "You're missing something, I think."

I looked down at myself. Nope, I'd remembered pants. "What?"

"This." She held out my shield.

I stared at it. She hadn't pushed all week, unlike Ray, and I was grateful for that. I didn't yet know what it was going to mean to me this time around, but I knew I wanted to find out. I took it and slipped the chain over my head. Angela adjusted it so it ran beneath my collar and the badge settled over my chest, close to my heart.

She gripped my arms with affection and nodded sharply. "Perfect."

I nodded back. "Let's do this."

We were led, by a thoroughly nondescript agent who didn't bother to introduce himself, through a series of corridors opening up into cube farms and offices with desks, people, and noise, not unlike the police station except folks were better dressed. We arrived in a long hallway with a series of rooms marked *Interview Room* followed by a number. There were unmarked doors between each interview room I could only assume were observation rooms.

When our escort opened the door to a brightly lit room at the end, SAIC Dennison and another agent, a young woman in a suit with tightly-bunned, mousy brown hair, rose from the table to greet us.

"Captain Curran, Detective Sorin, thank you for being prompt," Dennison said and motioned to the two chairs opposite them. "This is Agent Kincaid, our case analyst. She'll be keeping track of pertinent details as we work through the events."

I started to extend my hand, but she had already returned to her chair at the table to shuffle her file folders and stab at her tablet, acknowledging us with only a flicker of her gaze. Okay. Feds were weird.

A single rectangular table adorned with a pitcher of water and four glasses and four moderately comfortable chairs were the only furnishings. A camera in the upper corner of the room pointed at us and blinked red indicating it was on. The wall to our right was partially made up of one-way glass. Who was on the other side of that?

Angela clearly sensed my tension and poured water for us both so I didn't have to reveal my shaky hands.

"Let's get started," Dennison said without any further preamble.

It took everything I had to resist the urge to prop my head in my hands with a look of resigned annoyance, a la Hillary Clinton ten hours into the Benghazi hearing. But, I didn't rate like HRC, and it had only been three hours. It felt like three days.

It took me less than an hour to recount with as much detail as I could recall, the events beginning with the first time I stepped into Boomer's Billiards. Then we went over it again with questions. Then we went over it *again* with different questions.

The table was covered in paperwork and glossy photos. I stared at one of Mira dressed in leathers, coming out of Salon 603 downtown with her arm around Griffin Hillis. She was laughing, her freshly highlighted hair falling loose around her shoulders. She was beautiful.

"Detective Sorin, are you with us?" Dennison asked sharply.

My head jerked up. "Huh? Sorry. Yes, of course, sir. Um, what was the question?"

"Did you know it was Agent Van Allen that called in the tip from your gym that brought Officers Lyons and Neal to your location?"

"Uh, no. I didn't know she had done that."

"You hadn't discussed it? Made a plan?"

"No. Nothing like that."

"For all intents and purposes, by that point you and Agent Van Allen were partners? Would that be how you would describe your relationship?"

I couldn't help a laugh. "Reluctant partners, sure. But that's accurate, I suppose."

"And she left you. Alone and injured in the parking lot."

What the fuck? I straightened in my chair. I did not like where this was going. "To get the phone we needed to call for backup."

"But she didn't call for backup, did she? She called in an anonymous tip that brought Officer Lyons right to you."

"*She* discovered the mole in the department, which is more than I can say for anyone else." My gaze flicked to Angela. Her expression gave away little, but I could tell by the tightness around her eyes and set of her mouth she was angry. What the hell was this? Why were they going after Mira? Because they couldn't hold Albany PD responsible and they needed someone to take the fall for the botched operation?

"Indeed. Because *your* department"—his gaze flicked to Angela—"failed to realize you had not one, but *two* officers working for a known criminal organization." His expression remained impassive, but the smug smirk in his voice was unmistakable.

Despite the guilt and shame I knew she carried, Angela remained as cool as ever. "Let's stick to the case at hand, shall we, Agent Dennison? Unless you also want to schedule a meeting with your superiors, the Chief of Police and the Mayor to discuss why *your* office failed to keep Albany PD in the loop with regard to your operation extending well past the expected conclusion."

Is that what happened? Oh, shit. No wonder he's trying to deflect negative attention onto someone else. Over my fucking dead body would it be Special Agent Mira Van Allen. "What was the question, again?"

He cleared his throat and shuffled his papers. "In your professional opinion, did Agent Van Allen act appropriately in making an anonymous tip, in an effort to draw out the Rat Lords' operatives, instead of calling for backup using the phone with which Captain Curran provided you at the start of your assignment?"

"Yes," I said without hesitation. "There had already been multiple attempts on our lives. At that time, we didn't know if whoever was going to be on the other end of that phone was also going to be trying to kill us. She made the only decision she could."

"A decision that cost the life of Officer Neal and nearly yours as well."

Be cool. Be cool. My hands pressed flat onto the table. I tried to keep my voice measured. "The only people responsible for the death of Officer Brian Neal is Phil Lyons and the assholes he was working for. The *only* people."

He frowned. "If she hadn't made that call—"

"We wouldn't have known who in the department was on the gang's payroll." Nope. Nuh uh. Not cool at all. "She was undercover for a year. *You* were running this operation for *over* a year. And no one knew Lyons and Monroe were working for the Rat Lords. Meanwhile, you couldn't be bothered in all that time to check in with the new Chief of Police to make sure your operation was five by five with the locals? Agent Van Allen completed her op—*your* op. She saved my life. Repeatedly. And the life of my partner. Her dedication and sacrifice will save countless lives in this city and any other city that moves in Rat Lords' drugs and guns. You should be giving her a goddamn medal, not trying to hang her out to dry for your mistakes. This case is getting a lot of attention from the press and I will say that exact same thing to *anyone* who asks me about it. If you're looking for someone to blame because you lost the collar of your big-shot arms dealer, I suspect there's a mirror in the men's room."

Angela coughed.

"Sir," I added tightly.

I'd never fully appreciated the phrase "the silence is deafening" until that very moment. I stared at Dennison and he stared right back. Until he lowered his gaze to gather his papers, tap them into order and collect the photos from the table. Did I win? Does that mean I won?

"Thank you, Detective Sorin. Captain Curran. I think we have everything we need for now. Please, make yourself available should the ATF need to contact you again within the scope of this investigation. And don't hesitate to call my office if you have anything further to add." He quickly left the room with Agent Kincaid trailing behind.

Angela exhaled a deep breath. "That went well, I think."

My highly pleased-with-myself smirk was still in place up until I stepped out into the hall and right into the personal space of Agent Mira Van Allen leaning against the wall outside the observation room. Had she been in there? Her mixed expression of concern and gratitude said yes.

"Detective Sorin," she greeted and straightened off the wall with a grimace and sharp intake of breath. She wore the barest hint of makeup, her hair in a ponytail and her left arm in a shoulder-immobilizing sling strapping her arm across her chest.

Unlike most of the agents in different versions of the same suit, she was in what looked like government-issued athletic wear, all navy blue with ATF in bright yellow letters on her hoodie. Just as beautiful as ever.

Be cool. Be cool. "Agent Van Allen. You're well?"

"Not fit for duty for a while yet but getting better, thank you. You?" Her voice was breathier and it was clearly an effort for her to speak that many words at once.

"Um, same. Fit enough for desk duty beginning Monday."

"Pleased to hear it." She smiled softly. She looked past my shoulder and nodded. "Agent Looney will escort you out."

I followed her gaze where Angela was waiting with the same agent from earlier. No wonder he hadn't introduced himself. "Yeah, thanks. Um, when will I see…or *will* I see you again?"

She frowned and looked away for a moment. "It could be a while. This case is—"

"I get it. No need to explain." This sucked. Don't drag it out. "I'll let you get back to it. Take care, Agent Van Allen." I turned on my heel.

"Hey, Street Crimes," she called after me. When I turned back her eyes flashed wickedly and she mouthed my two new favorite words. "Rain check."

Angela graciously refrained from asking about my face-splitting grin and instead said, "Want to hit the gym tonight?"

Light legs, light arms and very light cardio were on the schedule, followed by lots of stretching. It was still brutal and I was flushed, sweat-soaked and totally wiped after an hour. Angela was three miles into her usual five-mile run on the treadmill. "Ang, I'm done. I gotta go before I end up having to curl up on a bench in the locker room."

She slowed her pace by half but didn't stop. "Just give me a few minutes of cooldown and I'll drive you home."

"Nah, it's okay." I checked my watch. I could catch the eight forty-five if I hustled. "I kinda got used to the bus. New me, new carbon footprint."

I raced through my post-workout routine and slammed my locker. *My* locker, *my* membership. It was one small thing

I could do to start to connect to the world around me. Angela was fast-walking her last mile by the time I raced by with a wave goodnight.

I didn't have a jog in me or even a fast walk, but I did have five minutes to get across the parking lot to the bus stop. It was dark but there were still quite a few parked cars and a few people coming in for last minute shopping in the plaza.

I shimmied between two pickups at the end of the lot. Emerging on the other side, something heavy and hard slammed into my gut, emptying my lungs and doubling me over onto the pavement with a grunt. It slammed into me again, between my shoulder blades, flattening me the rest of the way onto my face. I groaned and drooled, sucking at gravel and cigarette butts, trying to get my breath back.

"Fuck you, you lying piece of pig shit! I vouched for you!"

Oh, Christ. I rolled my eyes up to Tommy Pringle standing over me with a very large wrench, looking an awful lot like he was going to bury it in my skull. I raised a shaky hand. "No... Tommy...don't."

He was frothing, spittle flying out with every word. "Been following you for days. Just waitin' for my chance to hurt you."

I grimaced and gasped for every breath, but I managed to push myself back against a truck and prop myself up slightly, keeping one arm between us and one arm across my midsection. "We were...never looking for you, Tommy. You're free to go... just walk away."

"Go? Go where? Chumps? Boomer's? It's all fucking gone, thanks to you. I got nothin'." He raised the wrench again.

"You had your freedom," Angela said icily as she stepped out from between the trucks, weapon aimed at his chest. "Now, that's gone, too. Drop it. Down on your knees."

Tommy's eyes narrowed and his lip curled menacingly, but he dropped the wrench, raised his hands and knelt down. He may be angry and stupid, but he didn't appear to be suicidal.

"Patrol cars are on the way," Angela said, her eyes flicking to me briefly. "Lucy, talk to me. How badly are you hurt?"

I groaned and pressed around my gut. Tender, but nothing else. "Nothing broken, nothing bleeding."

"Stay there until the paramedics get here."

"Yeah." I pushed myself into a more comfortable sitting position, but that's about all I had the energy for.

"We're happy to take you in for an x-ray, but I don't think it's necessary, Detective. Your blood pressure is good, your sutures held up fine and there's no swelling or tightness in your abdomen. But you're going to be pretty sore for a while." The paramedic rolled up his blood pressure cuff and stowed it in his kit.

"Story of my life these days." I pulled the blanket tighter around me as I sat in the back of the ambulance while Angela finished up with the one remaining patrol car. Sweat had chilled my skin and adrenaline wore off about the time Tommy Pringle got hauled away in cuffs, gone from my sight and my life, but leaving me cold and shaking. My head dropped heavily into my hands. This is not how I thought my day was going to end, but at least it wasn't the end of my days. I snorted a painful laugh at my own stupid inner monologue.

"Lucy?" Angela sat perched next to me. "Talk to me."

I had liked Tommy. "He wasn't one of the bad guys, Ang."

Angela put a comforting hand on my leg. "They're all bad guys, Lucy. He may not have pulled a trigger or lit a match, but he supported those who did. At the very least he looked the other way and that makes him complicit."

"Yeah." She was right. She always was. He didn't deserve my sympathy or regret. None of them did.

"You ready?" She wrapped an arm around me. "You're coming back to my place. No arguments."

"You'll get none." I stood wearily with her help and gave her a grateful smile. "Thanks, Ang."

CHAPTER TWENTY-FOUR

"Hey, Lucky." Ray jogged to catch up with me on the sidewalk outside the station. "How'd your firearms requals go?"

"Ninety-three percent, baby. You?"

"Damn it. Beat me by two points. Glad I didn't put money on it again."

Sweet baby Jesus, why did everything have to make me think of Mira today? It'd been two months since I last saw and spoke to her at my debrief—and then nearly got killed, again. Monroe was pleading out and cooperating with ATF's investigation in hopes of a lighter sentence. Cops in prison did not fare well. Lyons was going down for Murder One of a police officer. No deals were going to be cut for him.

With the information Mira collected and corroboration from Monroe, twelve additional Rat Lords' club members had been arrested, including all the officers and Boomer. Charges were still being handed down and whoever was still free had scattered to the four winds to avoid getting swept up in the fallout. Tommy Pringle could have made that choice instead of trying to brain me with a wrench. Now he was gonna be doing ten to fifteen for aggravated assault. Chumps was condemned. The pool hall was shut down and the contents confiscated. All the tables and Harleys left behind were going to be auctioned off.

That was all well and good, and I was more than happy to move on. Well, maybe not happy, but then this morning every time I turned around, I slammed up against something that brought Mira to mind. First, Angela asked me to represent the women and try out some new concealable, flexible body armor the department was looking to purchase. Turns out I was already familiar with the vendor. I knew it was comfortable and Mira proved it could stop point-blank rounds. Ten out of ten would recommend.

Then I took a walk to the grilled cheese food truck for lunch. I jumped when I heard the rumble of Harleys, my hand going to my weapon, relaxing only when I realized it was an afternoon ride by a few members of the local chapter of Devil Dolls Women's MC. They were so badass—and law abiding— but I was happy to admire them from afar just the same.

"You headin' to the bar?" Ray asked.

"Yeah, seems like a nice night for a beer. Maybe a game or two."

Friday night end of shift and Copper Jack's was packed with the usual crowd and the music was loud. Cops, badge bunnies, and a smattering of businessmen and college kids were out in full force. Some bellied up to the bar, some played pool, and many trickled back and forth between inside and the recently finished back deck with picnic tables and strung lantern lights.

Ray headed to the bar. "Beer?"

"Yup." The back room was so full I couldn't see the tables through all the bodies. Bummer. Was hoping to have some fun tonight. Hope all those dudes weren't lined up to play.

Ray pressed a cold beer into my hand. "What's the occasion?"

"Dunno," I shrugged and sucked on my bottle. There was an unusual level of enthusiasm coming from the spectators in the form of hollering, shit-talking and bet-making. The crowd grew quiet enough to hear the strike of the cue, the crack of a ball, the ball off one rail and cleanly into the pocket. The crowd erupted in cheers. I admired the winner's finish. "Like it had eyes."

"Thank you, next!" a woman's voice raised over the din.

I froze with the bottle halfway to my lips. That was not just any woman. I would know that silvery smoky voice anywhere. Mira Van Allen was in the house and my heart pounded with excitement and nerves. Be cool. Be cool. I thrust my beer at Ray and pushed my way through the men lining the table.

She leaned up against the far wall, stick in one hand and beer in the other, laughing with a couple of patrol officers whose names I didn't even try to remember. Faded jeans, well-worn gray ATF T-shirt, black boots and a wide black leather belt with her badge clipped on. Her hair was back in a loose clip with strands framing her face. If I was still holding my beer I would have dropped it. God, give me strength. "I'm next."

The conversation stopped and all eyes were on me, including hers. Her gaze cruised me slowly, making a show of it. As luck would have it, my pants fit well, my white tee was tight, and as if ordained by the gods, I had on my good bra. She for sure noticed and her mouth quirked into a half-smile. "Rack 'em."

She moved around to the end of the table and waited, her eyes never leaving me while I gathered the balls. I held her gaze while I filled the rack and lifted it carefully.

She chalked her cue and bent over, giving me a clear view down her shirt. Probably all her bras were as lovely as the satiny black one I admired now. With an appreciative brow raise I made sure she knew I was staring. She grinned, pulling the cue back and forth between her fingers slowly before striking the cue ball and sending the balls to all corners of the table with a sharp crack, dropping a high and low ball each.

I nodded in approval. It hadn't really occurred to me Mira would be able to play, but she was amazing at everything else and she had spent a year living in a pool hall. She went for low-balls and her next shot took her right in front of me. I didn't move and her ass brushed against my thighs, sending a jolt of arousal from my belly on down. She didn't seem to mind and I sure as hell didn't. She dropped the seven leaving herself a clear shot at the two. "Nicely done."

"Thank you." She eyed me from beneath long lashes as she chalked her cue again before lowering herself over the table to make short work of the one and five.

I smirked as the cue ball rolled behind the thirteen, leaving her unable to see the four. "Unlucky."

She took a hopeless shot at it, doing her best to leave me stitched, then moved back to lean against the wall to reclaim her beer, taking a long slow drink from the sweating bottle.

I moved around the table to stand in her space, close enough to feel the heat of her body and smell her shampoo. I smiled sweetly. "You're using my favorite house cue."

"Am I?" She eyed it. "Pick a different one."

"I don't want a different one. I want that one."

"Tell you what. You let me use this one." She set her beer down and turned her back to me to reach beneath the table and pull out a black leather case. My black leather case. "And you can have this one."

"What?" I took it from her and unzipped the top. My AF8 slid out into my hands, smooth and undamaged. "How?"

She grinned behind her bottle and shot me a wink that nearly stopped my heart.

I was smiling like a kid on Christmas morning and didn't even care. I screwed my cue together and ran the shaft back and forth through my fingers, enjoying the feel of it. "Thank you," I whispered.

"I never thought I'd be jealous of a pool cue," she mused, watching me stroke it, "but here we are."

I laughed and chalked my cue. "I hope you don't think I'm gonna go easy on you."

She arched a brow. "Actually, I'm hoping just the opposite."

Oh, god. If pool foreplay wasn't already a thing, it was now. I resisted the urge to tug at my pants that suddenly felt too tight and returned my attention to the game.

It was my turn to show off. Mira stood still against the wall and watched me with a hooded gaze, the only part of her moving was her eyes as I walked around the table. Thirteen in the side, ten in the corner, twelve all the way down, nine in the side, fourteen in the side, and finally, fifteen in the corner, with draw to bring the cue all the way back down the table for a shot on the eight.

It didn't come back far enough. My gaze flicked to her and she pressed her lips together and raised her brows in challenge. She knew I was in trouble.

She moved to the end of the table ensuring she was right in my line of sight as I stretched to place my bridge hand, my right leg off the ground to give me a little added length. I slid the cue back and forth twice and took my shot. The cue ball struck the eight, firing it into the corner, before dribbling into the opposite corner with a thud. Scratch.

I rested my forehead against the cloth for a moment before straightening up off the table. "Oops."

Mira's eyes narrowed. "You did that on purpose."

"What? I would never." I unscrewed my cue. "Can I buy you a drink, Agent Van Allen?"

She seemed to consider my offer for a moment. "Got anything to drink at your place, Detective Sorin?"

"Where are your keys?" Mira gasped, running her hands up and down my body, front and back in the most arousing pat down ever. She leaned against me, her breasts pressing into mine, her mouth on my neck. Oh, god.

"Here...got it." I fumbled with the key and we stumbled in, tearing at each other's clothes. I pushed her up against the door, slamming it closed, and shuddered when her hands slid up beneath my shirt and under my bra to thumb my nipples. I untangled a hand from her hair to engage the deadbolt.

I let go of her long enough for her to rip my shirt off over my head then tugged at her belt, my mouth devouring hers with bruising passion. The buttons of her fly popped open and I slid my hands down her hips and over her ass, hooking her bikinis and pushing them down with her jeans along the way.

She gasped, dropping her head back against the door and gripping my shoulders for balance when I made my intentions clear and dropped to my knees. My hands ran up and down her body—her belly, the curve of her hips, the tensing muscles of her ass. I could smell her desire for me as my tongue trailed a path from her navel to her inner thighs, my nose brushing trimmed curls. I'd never been so wet and aroused in my life. The ache between my legs was nearing painful when she stepped out of her pants and spread for me. She trembled, her knees buckling at the first touch of my mouth on her.

She sucked in a breath. "I don't think…I can…"

I wrapped my arms around her, taking some of her weight, and murmured around my mouthful, "I've got you."

She drove into me harder, one hand clawing into my shoulder and the other flying out to knock the nude statue off the shelf by the door, shattering it. "Sorry…" she gasped.

"'S'okay." I grinned, encouraged by her panting gasps and quivering muscles. I teased around and around, up, down and in between, delighting in her increasingly desperate sounds as she shook in my arms. I closed my mouth around her clit, sucking and tonguing it hard until she bucked and cried out. I groaned into her as her explosive climax slickened my chin and filled my senses. So beautiful.

"Where did you…learn that?" She wrapped her arms around me and pulled me up to her, covering my mouth with her own, tasting herself on my lips.

I grinned, wiping her desire from my mouth with two fingers. "New York State Police Academy class of 2013."

I threaded one hand through her hair and the other raked her back beneath her shirt as we spun away from the door and pinballed toward the bedroom, laughing and gasping for air between teeth-clashing kisses. My new floor lamp crashed over, I stepped in the laundry basket I left out, and knocked off the clothes hanging from the bathroom door.

She popped the clasp on my bra and pulled it off. I whipped her shirt over her head. She ripped off my belt with a snap of leather before pushing me down onto the bed on my back and jerking off my pants. She stood over me, her expression sinister, as she unclasped her bra and let it slip down her arms to the floor. "Like what you see?"

Everything tightened, words failed me. So beautiful. She moved onto the bed on her knees, straddling me and pinning my arms by my head with a hand on each wrist. My back arched, my hips thrust toward her searching for contact, but she hovered just out of reach. I panted and struggled beneath her, but she held me firm. "Touch me, damn it."

"Shh." She kissed me softly on the lips, behind my ear, down my neck and across my collarbone. "I'm in charge, now."

I groaned, my eyes rolling as she worked her way down my chest and over to the first nipple, sucking it deeply into her mouth, stretching and flicking the tip with her tongue. A bolt of pleasurable pain shot through me, forcing my chest up to relieve the pressure. "Ah, shit…"

She smiled, letting my breast spring back and moving to the other side to lavish the other nipple with equal attention. I was on fire, writhing, panting, and sweating for her. She shifted her right knee between my legs, leaning forward and pressing into me. I thrust against her, searching for pressure and rhythm and her hips rocked with me, our legs intertwined. "Look at me," she rasped.

I dragged my eyes open to meet her gaze, bright with desire and a dash of amusement. She had me right where she wanted me—at her mercy—and she loved it.

My insides boiled, then melted, and boiled again. Mercifully, she let go of my wrists, hooked an arm around my waist and plunged two fingers deep inside me. I sobbed a breath and jerked wildly with every thrust until my body clenched and I came with a long gasping moan. Holy fuck.

She toppled off me and we lay sweating and panting atop tangled sheets. The room was filled with the sound of our heavy breathing, the smell of sex, and the heat from our efforts. After a while, I raised a wobbly leg. "My socks are still on," I murmured.

She snickered. "Mine, too."

"Are you sure there isn't anything you can't do?" I asked and reached for her hand, lacing our fingers together.

She started to laugh.

"What?" I rolled toward her. "What's funny?"

She turned her head so we were nose to nose. "I can't snap."

"Pardon?" I moved back so I wasn't only seeing her with a cyclops eye.

"I can't snap my fingers."

"Everyone can snap." I happily demonstrated several times with both hands.

"I can't."

"Try." I propped myself up on one arm.

"No. You'll laugh."

"I won't laugh. I promise." I laughed and she scowled at me. "Sorry. I'm sorry. I just had to get that out. I won't laugh again. Please, just show me."

Her mouth pursed into series of amusing shapes while she considered. Finally, she held up her right hand, middle and thumb pressed together in the pre-snap position. When she flicked her fingers there was just a swish of skin followed by a quiet tap against the pad of her thumb. "See?"

I fought a smile with everything I had. "Do it again."

She did it once more with the same result. It was so weird. She was doing everything right, there was just no *snap* in her snap. I couldn't hold it in any longer and grinned. "But you're so good with your hands."

"Shut up." She wrapped her arms around me and pulled me on top of her, our hot, sticky skin pressing against each other ignited my desire for her again. Hers as well, apparently, when she smashed her lips to mine and slipped her tongue in my mouth, devouring me before pulling away to say, "I think it's time for you to show me how good you are with *your* hands, Street Crimes. Rumor has it, you're 'smooth with the ladies.'"

"Oh, shit, you could hear me?"

"Every word."

"In that case." I stretched across her to the drawer in the nightstand and pulled out my cuffs. I dangled them in front of her narrowing eyes and widening smile. "Let me show you what else I learned in the academy."

EPILOGUE

I could hear footsteps, voices, and a child's squealing laughter. I knocked again, louder this time, knowing full well my first attempt to announce myself was bullshit, because I was nervous as hell.

The porch of the cute ranch in a well-maintained suburb of Syracuse was crowded with a porch swing, a couple of weather-worn chairs, a balance bike, stroller, and chewed sticks. The laughter stopped and there was a quiet murmur and steps toward the door. My heart raced and mouth went dry. I hoped I looked unthreatening.

An attractive woman with long brown hair in a ponytail, yoga pants, and oversize T-shirt, opened the door partway, keeping a barrier between us. "Hello."

A toddler clung to her leg with wide eyes and a sticky face. A block-headed black lab, totally uninterested in the stranger at the door, tried to lick the goo off the child's face.

"Hi." My voiced cracked embarrassingly. "Brooke Dolan?"

"Yes?" Her gaze darted over me, widening at the badge and gun. I kept my expression as pleasant as possible.

"I'm Detective Lucky Sorin with Albany PD. You're not in any trouble," I added cheerfully when she tensed visibly. "Do you have a few minutes to speak with me?"

"Babe, who is it?" a man's voice called from within the house.

"The police," she replied without taking her eyes off me.

An equally attractive man wearing a baseball uniform appeared behind her and scooped up the child who squawked and kicked little legs at being picked up unwillingly. He took me in at a glance. "What is this about?"

I gave him a nod of greeting and cleared my throat. "I was hoping to speak with Ms. Dolan about her sister, Skyler Kingston."

Brooke paled dramatically and his hand immediately went around her in support. Oh, thank god. He knows everything and I'm not outing any family skeletons. And he's maybe a nice guy. Good for her.

"Um, yes, of course." She stepped out onto the porch. "I'll just be a few minutes," she said to the man.

He looked concerned as he juggled the tot and shot a leg out to keep the dog from following her outside. "You want me to come?"

She smiled at him. "I got it. Thanks, babe." She closed the door behind her and gestured to the porch chairs. "This okay?"

"Yes, sure." I let her sit first and pulled the other around to face her before I sat. I gave her a few moments to collect herself and work through her own nerves by picking lint from her shirt, smoothing errant hairs, adjusting the faded chair cushion and looking anywhere, but at me.

"Are you here to tell me she's dead?" she whispered, finally making eye contact.

I swallowed hard. It was still hard sometimes for me and this woman was hearing it for the first time. "Yes. I'm sorry."

She nodded sadly but didn't cry. "How?"

"It was an accidental drug overdose about six months ago. I'm sorry we couldn't let you know sooner, but without knowing your last name, it took a while to track you down. In fact, prior to a few days before her death, I didn't even know Skyler had a sister." It was murder, but those responsible had been brought to justice. I had given a great deal of thought to how much I would tell Brooke Dolan about the life and death of her only sister. I wouldn't lie to her, but in the end decided I wouldn't go out of my way to offer information about Sky's involvement with the Rat Lords.

She looked up. "You knew her?"

I smiled wistfully. "I did. A little, I think."

"What was she like?"

The hard part was over and I relaxed finally, sitting back in the chair, crossing my legs. I wasn't here in a professional capacity, not really. Just a friend of her little sister sharing some memories—sharing a connection. "She was funny and smart. She could also be snarky and prickly as hell. She had more than her fair share of struggles but she never let that crush her. She tried really hard to make something better for herself. She wanted more and she was willing to work for it, you know."

Brooke laughed. "Yeah, I, um, don't remember everything, and I don't want to, but that sounds like Sky."

Maybe I was wrong. Maybe *this* was the hard part. Emotion tightened my chest and I sat forward again, elbows on my knees. "The last time I saw her…a few days before she died…she, um, asked me to help her find you. She wanted to reconnect with you."

Brooke sucked in a breath and blinked back tears. "I should have looked for her. I never even looked for her."

Girl, same. I reached across the space between us and took her hand. "You were kids. You didn't do anything wrong." My gaze swept over her and then her house. "You look like you've made a really great life for yourself. Good partner, beautiful child, goofy dog."

She laughed through the tears that had started to fall. "Yeah."

"Sky would have been really proud of you, I think." Tears pricked behind my own eyes. Damn it. I pulled the necklace from my pocket. "And she would have wanted you to have this."

Brooke stared at it a moment before her hand flew to her mouth to cover a sob. Tears streamed as she grasped the necklace with trembling fingers.

Her husband had to have been watching from the front window because he came out glares blazing, clearly thinking I had said something to upset her. I guess I did, I don't know. It was time to go, anyway. I pulled a card from my wallet and left it on the chair. "Don't hesitate to call me if there's anything you… anything at all."

As soon as I was far enough away that I thought they wouldn't hear me, I sucked in a shuddering breath, my own tears falling as I walked down the block to the car. The trees were vivid fall colors and the air was crisp. My T-shirt and sweater combo was begging for another layer soon. A blazer maybe?

My unmarked was right where I left it, and the woman I left in it was now leaning against the driver's side door, a blue ATF windbreaker to keep her warm. Her sunglasses were pushed up on her head, so I could see her sparkling eyes. She opened her arms and I fell into them, holding her tight around the waist while she hugged me hard—keeping each other warm.

"You okay?" Mira whispered into my hair, running her arms up and down my back.

"Yeah." God, she felt good. "Thank you for coming with me."

"Of course." She squeezed me harder before pulling away a bit and tilting my face to her with a finger hooked beneath my chin. She placed the softest, sexiest kiss on my lips. "I obviously had to come to make sure the personal information and location of a private citizen searched from a Federal database didn't get misused."

I sighed theatrically. "You're an ass."

"You love my ass."

"It's true. I do love your ass."

Bella Books, Inc.

Women. Books. Even Better Together.

P.O. Box 10543
Tallahassee, FL 32302
Phone: (800) 729-4992
www.BellaBooks.com

More Titles from Bella Books

Mabel and Everything After – Hannah Safren
978-1-64247-390-2 I 274 pgs I paperback: $17.95 I eBook: $9.99
A law student and a wannabe brewery owner find that the path to a
fairy tale happily-ever-after is often the long and scenic route.

To Be With You – TJ O'Shea
978-1-64247-419-0 I 348 pgs I paperback: $19.95 I eBook: $9.99
Sometimes the choice is between loving safely or loving bravely.

I Dare You to Love Me – Lori G. Matthews
978-1-64247-389-6 I 292 pgs I paperback: $18.95 I eBook: $9.99
An enemy-to-lovers romance about daring to follow your heart, even
when it's the hardest thing to do.

The Lady Adventurers Club - Karen Frost
978-1-64247-414-5 I 300 pgs I paperback: $18.95 I eBook: $9.99
Four women. One undiscovered Egyptian tomb. One (maybe) angry
Egyptian goddess. What could possibly go wrong?

Golden Hour - Kat Jackson
978-1-64247-397-1 I 250 pgs I paperback: $17.95 I eBook: $9.99
Life would be so much easier if Lina were afraid of something
basic—like spiders—instead of something significant. Something like
real, true, healthy love.

Schuss – E. J. Noyes
978-1-64247-430-5 I 276 pgs I paperback: $17.95 I eBook: $9.99
They're best friends who both want something more, but what if
admitting it ruins the best friendship either of them have had?